Dear Reader,

Do you have a secret fantasy? Everybody does. Maybe it's to be rich and famous and beautiful. Or to start a no-strings affair with a sexy mysterious stranger. Or to have a sizzling second chance with a former sweetheart.... You'll find these dreams—and much more—in Temptation's exciting new yearlong promotion, Secret Fantasies.

Kate Hoffmann is a master of rollicking, romping romantic comedies, and *Never Love a Cowboy* proves it. When Josie, a pampered celebrity, starts a new life with Travis, a bad-boy rancher, her ultimate secret fantasy comes true. But she soon realizes that roughing it on a ranch—even with a gorgeous cowboy—has its drawbacks!

In the coming months, look for Secret Fantasies books by Tiffany White, Madeline Harper and Mallory Rush. Please write and let us know how you enjoy the "fantasy."

Happy Reading!

The Editors

c/o Harlequin Temptation
225 Duncan Mill Road
Don Mills, Ontario
M3B 3K9
Canada

Dear Reader,

When it comes to secret fantasies, I have a few of my own. And one of those fantasies is to meet a hero like Travis McKinnon in *Never Love a Cowboy*—a tall, dark, handsome cowboy, a bad boy with a good heart. But since Travis exists only on the pages of this novel, I was forced to introduce him to Josie Eastman, a heroine worthy of this fantasy man. And in keeping with the Secret Fantasies series, I gave Josie a secret fantasy of her own.

When I developed the idea for *Never Love a Cowboy*, I wanted to show ranch life the way it really is. Though Castle Creek isn't the Hollywood ideal of an Arizona cattle ranch, it *is* based on reality—the wide-open landscape, the ramshackle buildings and the lack of indoor plumbing! What better place for a high-minded celebrity and a down-to-earth cowboy to fall in love?

I hope you enjoy Travis and Josie's story. I love to hear from my readers, so please write.

Sincerely,

Kate Hoffmann

# Travis couldn't sleep with her in the next room

He kept envisioning Josie's sweet little body clothed in his favorite flannel shirt. Finally, he grabbed his boots from the floor and flung open his bedroom door, then strode through the living room.

Josephine pushed up from the couch and blinked sleepily, her gaze following him across the room. "Where are you going?"

"I've got work to do," he muttered. "Where's my jacket?" Travis headed toward the kitchen, where he found it. He also found her underwear hanging from the towel rack. Travis touched the silky fabric and an unbidden image of her naked body appeared in his mind.

With a hiss of frustration, he headed back to the living room to collect his hat.

"Do you realize it's three o'clock in the morning?" she asked, brushing her rumpled hair from her eyes. "How are you going to work in the dark?"

Travis stared down at her. He was right. This pampered woman wouldn't last a week on the Castle Creek ranch. She was too beautiful, too privileged to spend her life in the desert. But he was not going to take the time to find out for sure.

Because if he did, he might never want this lady out of his life.

**Kate Hoffmann** has written eight wonderful novels for Temptation, and *Never Love a Cowboy*, like all her other titles, includes the unique blend of humor and warmth that has made her books more and more popular with readers. This book also has the added bonus of a bad-boy cowboy as a hero. Kate is single and still looking for her real-life Temptation hero. She lives in Milwaukee, Wisconsin, with her computer, her thesaurus and two cats.

## Books by Kate Hoffmann

HARLEQUIN TEMPTATION
456—INDECENT EXPOSURE
475—WANTED: WIFE
487—LOVE POTION #9
515—LADY OF THE NIGHT
525—BACHELOR HUSBAND
529—THE STRONG SILENT TYPE
533—A HAPPILY UNMARRIED MAN

# NEVER LOVE A
# COWBOY
## Kate Hoffmann

# *Harlequin Books*

TORONTO • NEW YORK • LONDON
AMSTERDAM • PARIS • SYDNEY • HAMBURG
STOCKHOLM • ATHENS • TOKYO • MILAN
MADRID • WARSAW • BUDAPEST • AUCKLAND

To my editor, Susan Sopcek, for her unerring instincts
and gentle guidance, and for finding me a "spot," a feat
deserving of ten dedications!

ISBN 0-373-25646-9

NEVER LOVE A COWBOY

Copyright © 1995 by Peggy Hoffmann.

# 1

"I NEVER THOUGHT I'd say this, but being a princess really sucks."

"Is that any way for royalty to talk?"

Josephine Eastman stuck out her tongue at Misha's reflection in the mirror. She had liked Mikhail Petrovych much better when he could barely speak English. Now that he had command of the language, he didn't hesitate to use his newfound vocabulary to tease and torment her.

Misha wagged his finger at her. "Who taught you to make such a pretty face, Josephine? The queen?"

"Thank you, Sigmund Freud," Josie said, shoving her tiara onto her head. "Finally someone who agrees that my mother is to blame for everything miserable in my life."

"Stop complaining, *Pavla*," he scolded, his accent heavy but his grammar perfect. "You are boring me with your whining." *Pavla* was his nickname for her. He had told her once it was the Russian equivalent of brat or snot, but Josie imagined the name was meant to be affectionate rather than insulting.

"You have no idea what it's like to be perfect, Misha," she teased. "I smile until my face feels like it's going to crack into a million pieces. I wave at everyone like they were my favorite Aunt Bess come to visit. I wear this stupid tiara even though it pinches my head. And all this tulle and satin is enough to send a debutante into an apoplectic fit."

"You get to travel this wonderful country, you wear pretty gowns and appear before thousands of cheering people. And they *pay* you to do it. You have what every little girl in this country wants and all you do is complain like a child."

Josie stared at herself in the mirror. So maybe she was being childish. But didn't she have a right? After all, she'd never had a real childhood. She'd spent every available hour since the time she was four years old freezing her butt off inside an ice rink, with coaches telling her what to do and trainers telling her when to do it. And after her backside had been properly refrigerated, her mother took over outside the rink with her own special brand of pointed advice.

Her eyes took in her surroundings. Every little girl's dream? She was sitting in front of a cracked mirror in a locker room that smelled like sweaty old socks, in the leaky basement of an arena in who-knows-where. If this was every little girl's dream, she'd hate to see a nightmare.

"Look at this place. I think I have a perfect right to complain, don't you?"

"You are not being truthful with yourself, *Pavla*," Misha replied softly. "It is not this place that is your problem."

"All right, Sigmund," she challenged. "Tell me what is."

"You are afraid," Misha said, his statement startlingly direct.

Josie stiffened, ready to jump all over Misha for his insult. But as she caught a glimpse of her reflection, she knew he was right. Every time she looked in the mirror, she saw exactly what he did, and what she hoped to hide from the world—a scared little girl who tried to be perfect but always came up short. Until now, she'd stubbornly refused to acknowledge that little girl.

"I am right, aren't I?" Misha said.

Josie closed her eyes and slumped back in her chair. "Maybe you are," she conceded. She knew he was. From the time her mother had shoved skates on her feet, she'd been terrified of failure. And the only way she could deal with her fear was to control it, to act like it didn't exist.

She opened her eyes, then toyed distractedly with her hair. "You know, I've never had control of anything in my life. Someone has always been waiting in the wings, ready to judge me, anxious to find me lacking. So I try to control whatever else I can. Is that so bad?"

Misha touched the mirror with his finger. "*Pavla*, if you are so unhappy with your life, change it. After all, this is America. Here you can be anything you want. Even president."

Josie laughed. "Right. That's exactly what our government wanted every Russian to believe before the wall fell. I hate to burst your Bolshevik bubble, Misha, but it's not true. For me, this—" She threw her hands out to indicate her surroundings. "This is as good as it gets. I'm trapped, just as sure as if I were imprisoned in some dreadful Russian goulash."

"Gulag. And I have told you before, Josephine, I am not Russian, I am Ukrainian. There is a large difference."

Josie looked around the dressing room wistfully. "I used to dream about all this when I was younger," she said. "The shiny medals, the pretty costumes, the ice shows. I'd lace up my skates and step out onto the ice and I'd feel like a real princess in a fairy-tale world. It was like a fantasy come true. But then, over time, the pressure got to be unbearable. Somewhere along the line, my fantasy just evaporated."

"Fantasy?" Misha asked. "Do I know this word?" He pulled out his little notebook and asked for the spelling, then wrote it down as Josie gave him each letter.

"Fantasy," Josie repeated. "It's like a perfect dream, something you want very much."

"So what is your fantasy now?" Misha asked.

"Lately I dream about running away from skating," Josie said, excitement tingeing her voice. "I dream about finding a place where I could just be alone and do exactly what I wanted. No David Garner telling me how to skate. No Evelyn Eastman telling me how to live."

"Do it," Misha said.

She shook her head and tucked a stray strand of dark hair under the tiara. "That's more easily said than done. I thought I could break free, after I won the medal. But by then I realized I didn't know how to do anything else. All I knew was skating. My mother made very sure of that."

"Your mother is not here, *Pavla*. She is at home in Connecticut. She cannot control your life anymore."

Josie rolled her eyes. "Oh, don't you believe that for a second. As long as I have skates on, Evelyn Eastman will be right there, standing behind me, pulling the strings."

"You need a plan," Misha advised. "*I* have a plan. I have financial goals and professional ambitions."

She scrutinized her reflection and sighed. "You're right. Look at me. I'll be thirty in a couple of months and I'm stuck skating the virginal Cinderella in a two-bit ice show. I'm living out of a suitcase. I should have a real job. Or I should be married with 2.5 children by now. I want a real life. A life of my own." She turned to Misha. "I could have a real life here in Cincinnati, don't you think? There must be something I could do."

Misha sat down next to her and gazed into the mirror. "I am sure you could, *Pavla*. But we are not in Cincinnati, we are in Arizona. Tucson, I believe."

"Tucson, Cincinnati, what difference does it make? Do you really think I could make a life for myself?"

Misha put his arm around her shoulder and gave her a friendly kiss on the cheek. "You could do anything you set your mind to, Josephine. Of that, I am sure."

Josie bumped against his shoulder playfully. "You're a good friend, Misha Petrovych. But you've got a run in your tights, and you forgot your eyes."

Misha picked up her eyeliner. Carefully, he drew a thin line below his left eye then surveyed his handiwork critically. He was her Prince Charming, a handsome and athletic skater, and her best friend. Like Josie, Misha had been an Olympic medalist in figure skating at Lake Placid. But unlike Josie, who had grown up in the lap of luxury, Misha had passed his childhood in Leningrad, where he'd trained.

Though Josie was considered as close to a princess as an American could get, Misha had the *real* royal blood pumping through his veins. His great-great-grandfathers and grandmothers had moved among the glittering courts of nineteenth-century Europe. Yet, to Misha, the hotel rooms and fast-food restaurants, the endless bus rides and frigid arenas, represented the good life. He was getting paid to do something he loved.

A knock at the dressing-room door interrupted their preparations. Josie grabbed her hairbrush and threw it at the door. "Go away, Richie," she shouted. "We're almost ready." Richie Brinker, the personnel manager, insisted that everyone gather in the wings right after warm-up for his corny pep talk. Josie preferred to skip the pep talk, hiding out in her dressing room until the overture echoed from the public address system, an artificial smile plastered on her face.

The door opened and Richie poked his head in. "Miss Eastman? Mr. Garner would like to see you."

Josie shot him a withering look. "Tell Mr. Garner that I'm in my dressing room preparing for a performance. He's welcome to speak to me here." A grin curled the corners of her mouth. It was always a good idea to reinforce her position as reigning diva. And refusing to jump to the director's bidding was all part of the game, a game her mother had taught her at a very young age.

*Go on, Josephine. You just walk right up to your toughest competitor and tell her that you love her costume. Tell her that the judges will love it, too. And then, as you turn away, laugh just a little so she will know that you didn't mean a word you said.*

*But, Mother, that would be cruel.*

*Do it, Josephine! All's fair in figure skating, darling, and you must work for every advantage. Believe me, your mother knows best.*

David Garner appeared in the doorway a few minutes later and Josie graced him with an alluring smile. As always, he looked like he'd just stepped off the pages of a men's magazine, his designer suit impeccably pressed, every hair on his head in its place.

"David, darling! What brings you down here to the bowels of this positively ghastly venue? Have you found me a better dressing room?"

He didn't return her smile. "Josie, I'd like to speak to you alone. Misha, you'll excuse us, won't you?"

Josie reached out and grabbed Misha's arm to prevent his escape. "Misha will stay," she said evenly in another play for power. "Whatever we have to discuss, David, I'm sure it can be discussed in front of Misha."

David nodded curtly. "All right, if that's the way you want it. We've decided to make some personnel changes, Josie. Tina will skate the Cinderella role from now on. We've assigned you the role of the wicked stepmother. Louise has your new costume. I'm sure you know the choreography... and the character should come naturally. She's waiting for you in the trunk room."

Josie forced a laugh, but her pointed glare telegraphed her true emotions. "Very funny, David. All right, so I missed a few rehearsals. I overslept. And I apologized to Richie for my little tantrum the other day. You don't have to threaten me. I'll be a good girl from now on."

"This isn't a threat, Josie. I've made a decision. You'll need to turn in your tiara and pick up your rubber nose and warts before we go on tonight." He glanced at his watch. "You've got thirty minutes. Don't be late." He turned and stepped through the door, then pulled it shut behind him, leaving Josie to stare after him.

"He's bluffing," Josie said, her voice brittle.

Misha looked over at her with a sympathetic smile . "I don't think so, *Pavla*. I heard him telling Tina this morning."

Josie shot out of her chair and paced the room. "You're wrong, Misha. You must have misunderstood."

She grabbed a jar of cold cream and hurled it across the room where it shattered against the door. The crash was followed by a string of vivid curses. "He can't do this! I am Josephine Eastman! I won a bronze medal in the '80 Olympics! I am America's princess."

"I'm sorry, *Pavla*. Maybe you can talk to David and change his mind. Maybe if you promise to—"

Josie held up her hand to stop his words short. Drawing a deep breath, she slowly shook her head. "No. This is it, Misha. If he wants some bimbo with a tight butt and a triple axel—a skater who possesses all the artistry of an elephant on ice—well, he can have her. I'm through with this princess garbage. I should have walked away from it ages ago." She stalked to the door, moving easily on the covered blades of her skates, the tulle flounces of her skirt rustling around her.

"You cannot quit, Josie," Misha said blandly, still occupied with his makeup. "You have a contract." Misha barely reacted to her anger. He'd experienced her tantrums before and had become immune to her histrionics.

Well, this was no tantrum, she was serious. "As far as I'm concerned, Garner can take his contract and shove it." She pulled the door open. "I'm outta here. Good luck lifting your new princess, Misha. I hope she isn't as fond of french fries as they say she is."

"You cannot just abandon me, *Pavla*," he said, worry beginning to creep into his voice. "Where will you go?"

"I'm going to find myself a life. Somewhere where there's no ice. Maybe it isn't too late for fantasies."

The slamming door reverberated through the dark airless corridors of the arena basement as Josie followed the pipes and cables to street level. She passed the wicked stepsisters who stepped back out of her path. She'd pissed off the stepsisters long ago and they knew not to mess with her when she was in a foul mood. As she was nearing the door to the street, David Garner called from behind her. Josie smiled. So he was prepared to apologize already. It hadn't taken him long to realize his mistake.

"Where the hell do you think you're going, Josie?"

Josie waved her hand over her head, refusing to turn around. "I'm quitting. 'Bye, David." She'd just scare him a little, pay him back for his foolish ideas. Wicked stepmother? In a pig's eye.

"Josie, come back here. That's our costume. We need that tiara for tonight's show!"

"Tough!" she shouted, shoving the door open and stepping out onto the street. She was nearly a block away from the arena when she realized that she was still wearing her skates. She also hadn't grabbed her purse or a coat. She shivered and rubbed her arms, trying to remember where she was. Hadn't Misha said they were in Arizona? It was awfully cold for Arizona.

"So much for running away," she muttered to herself. She'd have to go back to the arena, but she'd go back *after* the show had started. They would have to do without their damn tiara tonight. And they'd be short a wicked stepmother, as well. Biting back another curse, Josie continued down the street, not really watching where she was going.

She had walked for nearly five minutes when she heard the shout behind her. Turning, she caught sight of one of the show's truck drivers, Gus, a huge hulk of a man who also provided security for the show. She smiled smugly. So they wanted her back—bad enough to send Gus after her.

"Come back here, Miss Eastman. Mr. Garner wants his tiara!" Gus bellowed, lumbering in her direction.

His tiara? Seven years of her life dedicated to this damn ice show and all David Garner cared about was a tacky rhinestone tiara?

Josie turned on the toe of her skate and ran. She ran harder than she had in years. She ran until she was certain she'd lost Gus, then stopped and unlaced her skates. His plodding footsteps sounded in the distance as she pulled her skates from her feet. She continued her flight in her stockinged feet, tossing the skates into a trash can as she passed. Nine-hundred dollar custom-made boots. Nearly a year spent breaking them in. But she wouldn't need them anymore. She was through with skating for good.

Josie wasn't sure how far she'd run. A painful stitch twisted at her side and she stopped for a moment to suck in a deep breath of the cold night air. She listened for a moment, hoping to hear nothing. But the footsteps were there again. Frantically searching for a place to hide, she spotted a horse trailer attached to a battered pickup parked on the street beside her.

Grabbing the top edge of the trailer gate, she boosted herself up and over, tumbling headfirst into a pile of smelly straw. Layers of tulle billowed around her face and her tiara slid down over her eyes. She crawled out of the cloud of netting, beating it back with her hands and spitting straw from her mouth. "Try to find your tiara now," she muttered.

At least she was safe for a little while. All she needed was a few moments to rest and gather her thoughts. She also needed a plan. First she'd retrieve her purse with all her credit cards. After that she'd find a way back to the hotel for her clothes. Finally, she'd hop a plane for Europe or maybe she'd take a cruise, whatever her credit limit would allow, she'd do. As she pondered her options, she heard footsteps again, and then the slamming of a car door. She peered over the back gate. A car started and she slowly released her breath.

In that instant, just when she thought all her problems had been addressed, the trailer jolted into motion. Josie fell backward into the straw, her skirts flying up over her head. As she struggled to her knees against the swaying trailer floor, she felt something cold and wet press against her cheek.

Josie screamed as the trailer swung around a corner, sending her tumbling to one side, tangling her arms and legs around something four-legged and furry. The animal kicked and butted at her and bleated in alarm. A goat. She was sharing her hiding place with a smelly old goat. Josie scrambled to the opposite side of the trailer and hung on for dear life, waiting for the goat to attack and screaming for the driver to stop.

The truck and trailer gathered speed, rattling her teeth with every bump on the road. When she had fantasized about running away, this was not what she'd pictured! She'd pictured luxury hotels, first-class air travel, all the comforts she deserved. Instead she was cold, dirty, and traveling in a rolling barnyard.

Shivering, Josie settled back into the dirty straw, wedging herself into a corner for safety and pulling a canvas tarp over her for warmth. All right, so her plan had taken a slight detour. She'd just have to put it back on track. When the truck slowed or stopped, she'd simply hop out, hail a cab, and find her way back to the hotel.

But after what seemed like hours on the road, bruised and covered with dust and straw, Josie's fear began to overwhelm her. She pulled the tarp up under her nose and fought back a flood of emotion. What if the driver didn't stop? What if he . . .

She shook her head and consciously calmed herself. "He has to stop sometime," Josie said out loud, hoping the words would make it fact. "At least for gas." She tried to figure out how far they'd traveled and how long she'd been trapped in the trailer. But the minutes seemed like hours, and hours like days.

To Josie's great relief the truck finally stopped just as she had decided to risk jumping out the back at highway speed. The sound of the door opening and closing reached her. She struggled to her feet and peeked out, then crawled over the back gate. Her feet hit the ground and her knees promptly buckled beneath her. The whoosh of air from her skirt sent a cloud of dust up around her. Coughing, she pushed to her feet. When she realized the driver was not in sight, she stumbled aimlessly down the dirt street.

In the light of a single street lamp, she made out an unpaved road lined with a small gathering of run-down buildings. Above it all arched an endless black sky filled with stars. She turned to the sound of country music and the sight of a blinking neon beer sign, then headed toward the tavern—Javelina's, according to the hand-painted sign.

Josie sighed. First she'd have to figure out where she was. And then she'd have to find a way to get from where she was to where she wanted to be. That much of her rather sketchy plan was clear. She looked up and down the street then stepped up to the tavern door. She wasn't about to spend one more minute than she absolutely had to in a godforsaken ghost town on the edge of nowhere.

"TEQUILA," Travis McKinnon muttered. "And leave the bottle."

"Bad day?"

Travis shook his head. "No worse than every other day."

Jake slid the bottle and a glass toward him, then leaned his elbow on the bar. "Things not going so well at Castle Creek?"

Travis stared at the bottle, idly twisting it until the amber liquid caught the reflection from the mirror behind the bar. "I had to sell two horses today to pay for a new transmission on one of my windmills. I had just enough left over to make this month's payroll, pay the taxes and cover the vet's bill on that damn goat. Not one of my better days."

"It's the nature of ranching," Jake said.

Travis rubbed his forehead. Right now, the nature of ranching was giving him a splitting headache. "I've sunk nearly every penny of my savings into Castle Creek, trying to turn a profit. I don't know how my grandfather kept it running all those years."

Travis poured a measure of tequila into the glass and downed it in one gulp. His eyes watered and his breath stopped in his throat. After a year in the southwest, he still hadn't gotten used to the kick. Straight tequila in a chipped shot glass was nothing like the happy-hour Scotch and sodas he used to sip in Chicago fern bars.

"Your grandfather was a sharp old gristle heel," Jake said. "Smilin' Jack McKinnon knew that ranch better than he knew his own name. And he left Castle Creek in good hands."

"No one can run it into the ground quite like I can," Travis said, a sarcastic edge to his tone. "I just can't figure it out. I ran my father's multinational corporation and made a success of it. Why can't I run a simple ranch?"

"Ranchin' may look real simple, McKinnon, but it ain't. It's a tough life. Still, cow sense runs in your blood. Just give it time."

Travis rubbed the back of his neck, working at the knot that had developed on his two-hour ride home, a knot immune to the effects of bad tequila. "I don't have time. If I don't turn a profit by the end of this year, I'm headed back to Chicago. I made a deal with my father. If I couldn't make the ranch work, I'd return home and take my former place in the executive suite. He didn't pay for a law degree at Yale for me to be wasting my talents on a run-down ranch." The last sentence belonged to his father, not to Travis. He could still hear the words as clear as he had the night he'd told his father he was leaving the family business for ranch life in Arizona.

"Sounds like you grabbed the brandin' iron by the hot end on that deal," Jake commented.

Travis poured a second shot of tequila, then distractedly turned the bottle around and around between his palms. "Overconfidence, that's what it was. I was willing to agree to anything for a chance to come back to Castle Creek, to relive all the summers I spent there as a kid. All I've ever wanted to be was a cowboy. I never considered the possibility that I might fail."

"So don't," Jake suggested. "You own the ranch. Nobody can make you leave it."

Travis chuckled. "Being my father's son comes with a lot more strings than your typical American family. In addition to cow sense from my grandfather, I've inherited a big helping of McKinnon family duty. 'From his meager beginnings as a rancher's son to the top of the corporate world,'" Travis quoted. "Endless days at the office, all so his only son wouldn't have to scratch out a living on an overworked, overmortgaged piece of land." He paused, scraping at the bottle label with his thumbnail. "My father's right. If I can't make this work, I don't belong here."

"Give it time, buddy. Give it—" Jake's words died in his throat and he whistled long and low, his gaze fixed somewhere over Travis's left shoulder. "Well, lookie there. She ain't your typical cow bunny, now, is she?"

Travis turned slowly on his bar stool and followed Jake's stare. His eyes came to rest on a vision standing in the doorway. He blinked hard, then rubbed his eyes. What the hell had Jake put in the tequila? Travis reached back and grabbed the bottle, sniffed at it, then shook his head to clear his mind. But the hallucination refused to disappear.

Lord, he'd been way too long without a woman! That was the only explanation for his intense reaction to the dark-haired beauty entering the bar. Almost a year had passed since his former fiancée had deserted the ranch to return to her life in Chicago. Since then he'd thrown himself into his work, forgoing any female companionship. And for good reason—the last thing he needed in his life right now was a woman to complicate matters. But lately, when he didn't fall fast asleep from exhaustion, he had given himself over to a few very vivid fantasies.

But his fantasies always involved a tall, slender blonde with a minimum of clothing and a maximum of sexual experience, not a petite, raven-haired Tinker Bell lookalike. Travis rubbed at his eyes again. His fantasies had regressed to a very dangerous point. Maybe returning to Chicago wouldn't be such a bad idea.

He watched as the woman glanced nervously around the room. Taking a deep breath, she carefully began to weave her way through the drunken cowboys toward the bar. Travis couldn't recall ever seeing a woman in Javelina's.

"Hey!" Harley Carson shouted from his place near the jukebox. "It's a dad-blamed princess! We got ourselves a regular princess in Javelina's. Jake, I think this calls for a round on the house."

Leave it to Harley to notice her first. Travis's ranch hand loved to chase skirts even more than he loved chasing cows. Harley had started working with Travis's grandfather when he was fifteen. Besides Snake, Harley was the most experienced hand on Castle Creek, and after twenty-five years, Harley knew every inch of Travis's spread. And every pretty gal within a fifty-mile radius of Deadwater Gulch.

The rest of the cowboys turned their whiskey-blurred attention to Princess Tinker Bell, reaching out to touch her as she passed. She screeched as one ranch hand from the Bar M patted her on the backside, and she slapped at another wandering hand as she sidestepped the pool table.

When she finally reached the bar, she carefully straightened her tiara and smoothed her ankle-length skirt. Travis's gaze was caught by her delicate hands as they fluttered over the puffy fabric. Women's hands. He'd forgotten how beautiful they could be.

His gaze drifted over her wisp of a figure. She had the tiniest waist he'd ever seen, cinched by the blue velvet bodice of her dress. He was tempted to reach out and touch her, to skim his fingers along her perfect ivory skin, to twist a strand of her dark hair between his fingers, just to see if she was as warm and soft and real as she looked, or simply a tequila-induced illusion. He bit back a curse and reached for his second shot of tequila. If he knew what was good for him, he'd stay away from her—and any other woman that might happen into Javelina's.

He tried not to stare. Instead he caught himself drawing in a deep breath through his nose, needing to smell a female again for just a moment. He expected the scent of perfume to surround her slender body. But this wasn't any perfume he'd ever smelled. She smelled like a . . . a goat. Then she spoke and Travis forgot the pungent odor that surrounded her. Lord, she had a pretty voice. He slowly set the tequila down again without drinking it, turning his full attention to the princess.

"I—I'm looking for the owner of the pickup parked outside," she said, ignoring Travis and going directly to the bartender for help.

The cowboys quickly discarded their games of chance and sidled up to the mahogany bar. The princess watched them warily, the way a jackrabbit might watch a hungry coyote.

"I got a pickup," one of them said.

"So do I," another countered.

"Me, too," a third offered. "I got me a real nice pickup. You need a ride?" The princess shifted nervously on her feet. Travis sensed she was trying to decide whether to flee or turn and fight. But though these cowboys might get a little rambunctious in the presence of a "purdy gal," Travis knew they were basically honorable men. She had nothing to fear; chivalry was alive and well in the Arizona outback.

Jake's brow rose a few degrees as he leaned across the bar. "I'm afraid every guy in here tonight arrived in a pickup, Miss. You'll have to be more specific."

The men waited to hear what she had to say next. The princess bit her lower lip and frowned. "Maybe it would be best if I spoke to Javelina," she said softly.

Travis smiled. She pronounced the word with a hard *J*, like javelin, rather than with a soft *H*, typical in the Spanish language. She obviously wasn't from the southwest or she'd know how to say the word. And she'd know that Javelina wasn't a person.

"Javelina?" Jake asked.

"Yes. Javelina. The owner. Is she here?"

"I think you should let her talk to Javelina," Travis offered.

Jake turned and retrieved the tavern's mascot, a stuffed wild pig that stood guard over the cash register. The pig had been nearly two feet high at the moment of its untimely demise, and about as ugly an animal that the low desert had ever produced. And it smelled twice as bad as the princess herself. The bartender placed the bristly old *javelina* in front of her and her eyes widened. She crinkled her nose and stepped back.

Travis chuckled. "That's Javelina," he said, patting the pig on the back and sending little puffs of dust into the air. "You can talk all you want, but I don't think this here critter is going to answer you."

Travis watched her spine stiffen and a stubborn look settle on her features. For the only woman in a roomful of drunken cowboys, she certainly had a lot of pluck. She was at least half a foot shorter than the shortest cowhand and looked like she had all the strength of a newborn foal. But something in the set of her jaw and the narrowing of her emerald eyes told him that she was used to getting her own way.

She glared at Travis. "All right, then allow me to take a step down on the evolutionary scale and ask for *your* help," she said tartly with an aristocratic arch to her brow. "I've been brought here against my will by some idiot driving a red pickup and pulling a horse trailer. Now, if you'd point out the owner of the trailer, I'm sure the driver would be happy to return me to Tucson."

Travis smiled and shook his head. This was downright entertaining. Better than a good game of crack-a-loo, though for a city boy, Travis was getting rather adept at tossing his quarter up to the ceiling of Javelina's and dropping it right on top of the crack in the floor. Last Friday, he'd won nearly twenty dollars. Still, it usually wasn't hard to beat a bunch of roostered cowboys who had drunk more than a week's share of red-eye in one night. But he had to admit, a spirited discourse with a lady was much more fun than a game of chance with the boys.

Newt Parker, another of Travis's ranch hands, leaned over from the other side of the princess, his baby face alight with interest. "Ain't that your horse trailer parked out front, Travis?" he asked, squeaking out Travis's name. Though Newt was nearly nineteen, his voice still cracked now and then, especially when he was nervous—or in the presence of a girl.

Travis shot him a quelling look. "Yeah," he replied. "That's my trailer, Newt, but I didn't bring this lady into town. I'd have noticed her sitting next to me, don't you think?"

She crossed her arms and tapped her foot. It was then that he noticed she wasn't wearing shoes. "You *did* bring me here," she insisted. "In your trailer, with your goat."

He frowned. If she hadn't been inside his trailer, how did she know about Winnie, his nanny goat from hell? "What were you doing in my trailer?" Travis demanded.

She gave him an insolent look, then glanced over at Jake. "May I have a mineral water, please?"

Jake quirked a smile in Travis's direction and Travis rubbed his jaw in irritation. "Give the lady a mineral water," Travis ordered. He turned to her. "You've got a pretty educated thirst for a place like this."

She ignored him and watched as Jake opened the tap beneath the bar and filled a glass. He handed it to her and she sniffed disdainfully.

"It's got minerals in it," Jake assured her.

She took a leisurely sip, then made a great show of brushing the dust and bits of straw from her clothes. Travis knew exactly what she was up to. She was playing a little game, making him wait until she was good and ready to explain herself.

"That'll be a dollar," Jake said.

"For a glass of tap water?" she asked.

Jake nodded. "We're in the desert and we got a water shortage. And I don't make my livin' handin' out free water to everyone that's thirsty," he challenged. "Whiskey or water's the same price at Javelina's."

"Then forget the water. I'll take a whiskey," the princess said stubbornly.

"I'll buy that drink for her, Jake," Newt said.

"Her drink's on me," Harley said, pushing in between Newt and the princess.

They both slapped down a dollar, then wrestled over which one Jake would take. He finally took both. Travis ground his teeth. He'd sold two horses this morning to pay Harley's and Newt's wages and they were throwing their money away as though it grew like sagebrush on the desert.

Tinker Bell tossed the drink back like she'd been hanging out at Javelina's her whole life. But once the liquid fire hit her throat, her icy disdain melted before his eyes. She blinked back a flood of tears and tried to keep from coughing by pursing her lips together and taking deep draughts of air through her pert nose.

"Are you really a princess?" Newt asked, awestruck.

"Of course she's a princess," Harley said. "She's got a crown, don't she?"

"She could be a queen," Newt shot back. "Or maybe a fairy."

"Fairies don't wear crowns."

Newt snorted. "What makes you the big expert on fairies, Harley? You're just a crock-headed saddle stiff."

"And you couldn't teach a settin' hen to cluck," Harley retorted.

Travis couldn't believe what he was seeing . . . or hearing. Newt and Harley, like most of the cowboys who frequented Javelina's, were men of very few words. His grandfather had once told him that conversation was like building a campfire—a cowboy never used up all his kindlin' to get his fire started. Obviously, the boys thought this "princess" was worth a whole cord of kindlin' and then some.

The princess coughed, then cleared her throat. Travis's ranch hands turned their attention back to her.

"Are you hungry?" Harley asked.

"I'll buy you dinner," Newt offered.

The princess looked back and forth between the arguing pair. "No," she croaked, the whiskey still wrapped firmly around her voice.

The two cowboys appeared crestfallen.

"Wha—what I meant was, I'm not a fairy. Or a queen. But I am hungry and I'd love some dinner." She paused as if she were evaluating the two men. "And I actually am a princess. My name is Princess—Josephine . . . Princess Josephine of—" She smiled sweetly. "Well, you wouldn't know where it was anyway." She batted her eyes at the pair of cowboys, then turned to Jake. "What are your chef's specials tonight?"

Jake grinned. "Well, we got beef jerky, pickled eggs and chili."

Princess Josephine laughed as if Jake had made the most delightful joke she'd ever heard. "I think I'll take the chili. And after I've dined, Mr.—" She turned to Travis, but she didn't flutter her lashes at him. It was if she sensed it wouldn't do any good.

"McKinnon. Travis McKinnon," he said.

"Mr. McKinnon can drive me back to Tucson."

Travis opened his mouth, ready to tell her she'd best start walking, when the crowd of cowboys decided to lodge their own protest.

"You can't go!" Newt cried.

"We ain't never had us a real live princess in Deadwater Gulch," Harley added.

"Well, I'd truly love to stay," Josephine said. "This would be a wonderful place to . . ." She lowered her voice to a whisper and placed her hand on Harley's forearm. "Hide out. If you know what I mean." She gave them all a knowing look. Problem was, Travis mused, these cowboys had left their brains inside an empty whiskey bottle hours ago. They wouldn't know what she meant if she branded it on their buck-naked backsides. He figured she was probably on the run from a husband or a boyfriend. What he couldn't figure was the costume.

"Hide out?" Jake asked. "You wouldn't be runnin' from the law, now, would you? Deadwater Gulch is a law-abidin' town and we don't want any trouble here."

He placed a bowl of chili in front of her and the princess smiled. "Oh, no. There's just been a bit of trouble at the palace." She waved her spoon distractedly. "A nasty little coup. I'm afraid my life is in peril if anyone finds out where I am. You will all keep my appearance here a secret, won't you? You won't tell anyone if they come looking for me after I've gone."

Reassured by their obliging nods, she dug into the chili as if she hadn't eaten in days. But Jake didn't make his chili for the delicate constitutions of runaway princesses. His patrons all possessed one trait in common—an iron gut. The chili hit her worse than the whiskey. And the spoon hit the bar with a clatter as she frantically snatched up her glass of mineral water and gulped it down.

"I'm not driving you back to Tucson," Travis said bluntly, knowing she couldn't possibly talk back now. "You can forget that idea, Your Highness."

She gasped for breath, then finally found her voice again. "But—but you have to. You're the one who br-brought me here." She coughed once.

"And you're the one who was dumb enough to climb into my trailer. I'm dead tired and I've got a full month's worth of work waiting for me at my ranch. You'll have to find another chauffeur . . . Your Highness." The last was said with a liberal dose of sarcasm.

She narrowed her eyes and glared at him, then forced a sweet smile. "I'm sure one of these kind *gentlemen* would escort me back to the city."

"Seein' as how you're in danger from that palace coot," Newt said, "maybe it would be best if you stayed in Deadwater Gulch."

"I think that's a fine idea," Harley added. "What do you boys think? We don't want our princess to leave just yet, do we?"

The decision was unanimous. Every cowboy in the room shouted their approval. They all wanted Princess Josephine to stay a spell. It was obvious Travis wasn't the only man in Cochise County suffering through a drought of female companionship.

The princess waved her hand. "I—I would love to stay in your...lovely little town, but I don't have much money with me. I left . . . the palace rather abruptly."

"We'll find a place for you to stay," Newt offered.

"And don't you worry about payin'," Harley completed.

Travis knew what was coming next, but he couldn't speak fast enough to stop it.

"You can stay out at Castle Creek," Newt and Harley said in tandem.

"Oh, no," Travis said, holding up his hands. "We are not set up for houseguests."

"You brought her here, McKinnon," one of the Bar M cowboys shouted.

"Yeah, McKinnon," another cowboy called. "It's only right you should put her up at your place until you can take her back to Tucson."

"She doesn't have anyplace else to go, Travis," Newt volunteered. "Not tonight. And she'll be safe there with me and Harley to watch over her." He turned to Princess Josephine. "And you don't have to worry. We won't—well, you know." Newt blushed. "I mean, we'll be perfect gentlemen." The room rumbled with the crowd's assent and it didn't take more than an instant for Travis to realize that it wouldn't be wise to argue with a bunch of cowboys who had overindulged in tonsil varnish. If she didn't go home to Castle Creek, she'd go home to some other ranch. And he knew he could trust his cowboys better than he could trust anyone else's.

"Look's like you got yourself a houseguest," Jake chided.

"She's sleeping in the bunkhouse," Travis muttered.

"You put that woman in with your boys and you won't get a lick of work out of them come tomorrow," Jake commented.

Travis rubbed his tired eyes. He was tempted to walk out of Javelina's right then, forgetting everything that had transpired since the princess had walked in the door. He was tempted to drive her back to Tucson immediately, but repeating the four-hour round trip was the last thing he wanted to do. He was tempted to throw back that second shot of tequila and then polish off the rest of the bottle while he was at it. But he knew that he'd better keep his wits about him when dealing with the newly crowned princess of Deadwater Gulch.

In the end, he grabbed her by her blue-blooded hand and pulled her through the room and out to his parked truck. Hell, if she thought she was going to get the royal treatment from Travis McKinnon, she had another guess coming.

# 2

JOSIE CAST a sideways glance at Travis McKinnon as he shoved the key into the ignition and started the truck. Beneath the brim of his cowboy hat, his profile was outlined by the light glowing from the neon beer sign. She let her gaze drift along a furrowed brow, a straight nose and a firm jaw. She had to admit, he was handsome in a rugged but scruffy-looking way.

He wore a mud brown canvas coat with a leather collar, a plaid flannel shirt, and a pair of jeans so faded and worn the seams were nearly white. His cowboy hat matched his coat and hid his short-cropped hair, hair she remembered as deep chestnut, streaked with the sun and a little darker at the sides. A week's worth of stubble only added to his slightly disreputable appearance.

Josie stifled a giggle. Evelyn Eastman would be positively aghast if she knew her precious Josephine was consorting with a common cowboy. Josie's mother was always on the lookout for a prospective son-in-law. A doctor with a well-established practice was the preferred choice, but a reputable lawyer would also do. Someone, anyone, who could support her daughter in proper Eastman fashion.

Unfortunately for Evelyn, Josie didn't share her mother's predilection for conservative, wealthy men. Always wild and rebellious, Josie was attracted instead to the bad boys that her mother constantly warned her against. She'd even been married once—for two days, when she was seventeen—to a man who rode motorcycles for a living. Her mother had promptly had the marriage annulled. Dangerous men appealed to Josie, and right now, Travis McKinnon looked as dangerous as they came.

His chiseled mouth was drawn into a hard line, and his pale blue eyes, so brilliant in the hazy light of the bar, were now dark and humorless. Josie drew in a deep breath and sighed, hoping to get at least some reaction from him. But he merely shoved the truck into gear and floored the gas pedal, spraying dirt and gravel out behind them in a dusty plume. The trailer fishtailed, but he easily brought it back under control and they headed out of town.

The minutes and miles bumped by and Josie waited for him to speak. A country-western song wailed from the radio and he tapped his gloved finger on the steering wheel to the beat. When it didn't look like he was going to bother with conversation, she decided to make the first move. "Is your ranch much further?" she shouted over both the music and the wind rushing through his open window.

He didn't reply, his eyes fixed on the road, his mind somewhere else. Josie settled back into the seat and rubbed her arms with her hands. The cold night air buffeted through the truck, sending shivers through her body. She was used to the cold, after all, she spent hours every day on a sheet of ice in a costume better suited for sunbathing. But if she couldn't move, she couldn't keep warm. Pursing her lips, she tried to stop her teeth from chattering.

Cursing softly, he pumped the brakes and stopped the truck in the middle of the desolate road. At first, she was sure he was going to dump her off right there. But then, he twisted out of his jacket and tossed it her way.

"Thank you," Josie murmured, pulling it on.

The quilted lining still held the warmth from his body and she snuggled down into it. His jacket smelled like he did, fresh and clean, like the night air, and tinged with just a hint of something spicy. He smelled like a real man, not like one of those buttoned-down bachelors reeking of designer cologne that her mother paraded before her whenever she went home to Connecticut.

"So what's your story, Princess?" he said, putting the truck back into gear.

"My story?" Josie asked.

"Yeah. The real story. 'Cause I don't believe for a second that cud you were chewin' for the cowboys back at Javelina's."

She crinkled her nose. "Cud?"

"That bull about you being royalty."

"It's the truth," Josie said evenly. "I am a princess."

He laughed, a deep, rich sound that did nothing to shatter the tension that hung between them. "Yeah, right. So are you running away from a husband or the cops?"

"I am Princess Josephine Petrovych," she said. "And my great-great-grandmother was a cousin to Nikolai Aleksandrovich Romanov, Czar Nicholas the Second, of Russia." Josie went on to repeat the story she'd heard hundreds of times from Misha, twisting it slightly to suit her circumstances, but keeping the basic history and genealogy in tact. "So, you see," she said. "It's the truth."

Or at least part of it was, Josie thought. She considered telling him who she really was, but somehow she sensed that it would be best to keep her identity to herself, at least until she'd fully formulated her plan. Or until the revelation might prove more profitable than pretending to be a princess.

Travis shook his head. "A very pretty story, but I don't buy it."

"Tough toenails," Josie replied stubbornly. "It's still the truth."

"Tough toenails? Did they teach you that at princess school?"

"I don't care what you believe," Josie said, crossing her arms over her chest defensively.

"All right, tell me this. Where are your shoes?" he asked. "All the princesses I've ever met wear shoes. Crystal slippers, isn't it?"

"I—I lost them when I was running," she shot back. "And I seriously doubt that you've ever met a princess."

"Who were you running from?"

She paused. "Bad men. Very bad men. Enemies—of the crown. I—I don't know their exact names, but I know that they're bad."

A muscle in Travis's jaw tightened. "All right, don't tell me," he snapped. "It doesn't matter anyway. The next free moment I can find, I'm taking you right back to whatever funny farm you escaped from—enemies or no enemies."

"I'd sincerely appreciate that," Josie said. "The last thing I want is to be stuck out here in the middle of nowhere."

"And the last thing I need on Castle Creek is a damned woman," he muttered.

"Well, I don't want to be on Castle Creek, either," Josie said. She paused and looked out the window.

They hadn't passed a single house since they'd left Deadwater Gulch and the road had deteriorated to a mass of bumps and jolts, slowing the truck to a crawl. All she could see in the beams of the headlights were two dirt ruts and a few scraggly bushes on either side. The landscape was eerily invisible in the moonless night, with only the twinkling stars breaking the inky black expanse of the sky. "Where is this Castle Creek, anyway?"

"We're on it right now," Travis said. "We've been on it for the last ten minutes."

"I don't see anything," Josie said.

"What did you expect to see?" he asked.

"Cows, barns, maybe a house," she said.

"That's what you'd see on a farm, Princess. Castle Creek is a ranch. Thirty thousand acres. And you won't see cows. The cattle are out on the range. We don't keep four hundred head in a barn. And the house is just over the next rise."

"You own thirty thousand acres of land and four hundred heads of cows?" she asked. To Josie's disappointment, he didn't seem quite as dangerous now. He sounded like the kind of man her mother would love. But then again, who was to say that a bad boy couldn't own a little property?

Travis chuckled. "I don't own Castle Creek," he said softly. "It owns me. Heart and soul." The last was added almost reverently. Josie glanced over at him and considered his statement, so cryptic yet oddly poetic at the same time. Suddenly he didn't seem as distant and angry, merely exhausted.

She turned back to squint out the windshield into the dark. A ranch so big had to have a mansion for a ranch house. She imagined a massive, white-pillared home, a corral with beautiful horses inside it, maybe even a swimming pool. If Castle Creek lived up to its name, it might not be a bad place to lay low until she came up with her grand plan for how she'd start her fantasy life. She wondered if Travis had servants.

But any visions that Josie had of a luxurious ranch house resembling those in the movies were soon replaced by stark reality. A bright white light set atop a telephone pole illuminated a long, low, stucco building with a corrugated metal roof and a crooked porch that ran the length of the facade. A pair of gnarled trees and a ragged brown lawn provided the only landscaping. A few ramshackle sheds could be seen on the fringes of the yard.

Travis turned off the truck. "Welcome to Castle Creek," he said. "I know it's not the palace, but it's home."

An animal scurried out from under the porch and disappeared into the night. No, this definitely wasn't the palace. The palace didn't have creatures living under the front porch. "What was that?" she said. "A dog?"

Travis shrugged. "Just some critter. The dogs sleep in the barn or the coyotes get 'em."

"Coyotes?" Josie asked.

"They'll run down almost anything if it gives 'em a good chase. Except maybe a mountain lion."

"You have mountain lions *and* coyotes on this ranch?" Josie gasped.

Travis smiled and climbed out of the truck. "On occasion." He slammed the door and leaned in the open window. "They seem to come out just for houseguests, though. The last time we had company..." He paused, then shuddered. "Well, I don't like to think about that."

He started toward the house and with a tiny scream of alarm, Josie hopped out of the cab and hurried after him. She fell into step at his side, matching his long strides, and instinctively grabbed his sleeve along the way, as if he might offer some protection from the wild animals that lay in wait.

Travis looked down at her white-knuckled fingers and grinned. As if she'd been burned, she snatched her hand away. She was touching a perfect stranger! But the feel of his arm lingered in her memory: soft, well-worn flannel with hard, lean muscle and warm flesh beneath. An unbidden image of that arm wrapped around her waist, holding her against an equally hard, lean body—protecting her from the coyotes, of course—flitted through her mind and she stifled a moan.

She might be able to trust Travis McKinnon, but could she trust herself? There was no getting around the fact that he was handsome and sexy, and the only man she'd met in a long time that didn't wear ruffled shirts, tights, and eyeliner. Was it any wonder she found herself mildly attracted to him?

Travis climbed the stairs, then opened the front door. As she hesitated at the bottom of the porch steps, her gaze shifted from his wide shoulders to his narrow waist, and then to his backside. She tried to decide what he might look like in a pair of tights, but she needn't have bothered. His jeans fit almost as well, hugging his body until she could imagine every muscle, every curve, every inch of warm, hard—

Josie's fingers clenched convulsively at the thought. She dragged her gaze away, banishing the image from her mind. Travis McKinnon was dangerous, all right. He had no idea just how dangerous he really was. He was turning her normally sharp-witted mind to mush.

She wrapped his jacket more closely around her and glanced up to find him standing in the doorway, arms braced on either side of the doorjamb, his tall form silhouetted by the light from inside the house.

"Are you coming, Your Highness?" He swept his arm out and bowed mockingly. "Sorry, I forgot the red carpet, but it's at the cleaner's. Too many royal guests lately."

Swallowing hard, she placed her foot on the first step. Did she really want to spend the night in the same house as this man? After all, what did she know about him? Just because a bunch of cowboys gave him the Good Cowpunching Seal of Approval, didn't mean he wasn't some sex-crazed maniac ready to have his way with her.

"We're going to have to find you some crystal cowboy boots," he commented blandly. "Scorpions will bite right through those flimsy socks."

Coyotes, mountain lions and now scorpions. One thing she *did* know was that he seemed to be taking perverse delight in frightening her. She knew there were no scorpions in the United States. She frowned. Or was that tarantulas? Either way, she'd teach him not to tease her anymore.

"Ouch!" Josie cried, grabbing at her foot and crumpling onto the porch steps. The skirt billowed out around her.

He was at her side in an instant, fighting his way through the tulle. "What's wrong?" He ripped off his gloves and pulled her hands away from her foot. "Did something bite you?"

Josie bit her lower lip, not in pain but to keep from laughing, and nodded. "I—I think so. Ooooow, it hurts." She even managed a tiny tear and a whimper.

Maybe she should pencil a career as an actress into her life plan.

She expected him to help her to her feet, but instead he scooped her into his arms and carried her into the house. "What the hell are you doing walking around in the desert without shoes?" he scolded as he gently lowered her onto a threadbare couch. "I could have told you you'd get bit sooner or later." He gently removed her left sock, then tore away her pink tights, shredding them up to her knee.

"I guess it was sooner, huh," she murmured, wondering if she'd bothered to shave her legs that week.

Holding her ankle in one hand, he pulled off his hat and tossed it, brim up, on the coffee table. Then he bent his head over her foot. An exquisite tingle slowly worked its way up her leg as his fingers skimmed across her skin. She closed her eyes. Suddenly the game had turned serious and it seemed as if *he* were getting the better of *her*.

"Where did it bite you?" he asked, examining each side of her foot.

She took a shaky breath. "I—I'm not sure." *On my calf*, she wanted to say. *Or maybe it was on my thigh. No, I'm sure it was my left breast.* Right now, she was willing to say anything to feel his hands on her body for just a little longer, to enjoy the delicious and unfamiliar feeling his warm touch triggered.

"Here?" He pushed on the sole of her foot with his thumbs.

She winced as if in genuine pain. "I—I think so."

Suddenly her foot bounced on the couch and she opened her eyes. He stood beside her, his features hardened into an icy mask. "When your leg starts to swell to twice its size and you start foaming at the mouth, call me. I'm going to bed." He turned and walked away, his boots echoing on the rough plank floor.

"Wait a second! Where am I supposed to sleep?" she asked. "Where's the guest room?"

He slowly faced her. "You're looking at it, Princess. You sleep on the couch." He grabbed a wrinkled flannel shirt from the back of a chair and tossed it her way. "There are blankets and a pillow in that chest." He pointed to the far wall. "You can clean up in the kitchen sink. The outhouse is thirty yards due west from the back door. If you've got to go, take a flashlight with you. And the rifle," he added, almost as an afterthought. "And for God's sake, put on some shoes if you're going to walk around outside."

Josie gasped. "Outhouse? You mean you don't have indoor plumbing?"

He shook his head smugly. "What do you think this is, the Plaza?" With that, he stalked into his room, slamming the door behind him.

With a scream of frustration, Josie balled up the flannel shirt and hurled it in the direction of the bedroom, then slouched down into the lumpy couch. "The Plaza?" she shouted. "You wouldn't know the Plaza if it fell out of the sky and hit you on the head. I've stayed at the Plaza before, buster, and let me tell you, *they* know how to treat a guest."

The bedroom door opened and a robe and two bath towels came flying out, hitting her squarely in the side of the head. "Sorry, but we're all out of mints for the pillow," Travis called. "Have a pleasant night, Your Highness." The door slammed again.

She tossed the towels aside, then jumped off the couch and paced the length of the room. "This is just great," she muttered. "I spend two hours in a smelly old trailer with a goat that's determined to taste figure skater for the first time in its miserable life. Then I spend another entertaining hour in a tavern with a stuffed pig and a couple dozen drunken cowboys, enjoying a lovely two-course repast of chili and whiskey, a meal that could have melted paint. And now I manage to find myself staying in the only place on earth where going to the bathroom is a life or death proposition." She flopped back down on the couch again, sending a huge puff of dust up around her. This fantasy life was getting worse by the minute.

Josie waved her hand in front of her face, then sneezed twice. It was clear Travis McKinnon didn't believe in basic housekeeping. Every surface in the room, even the scuffed pair of cowboy boots in the middle of the braided rug, was covered with a thin coating of dust. Besides the couch, the postmodern dustbowl decor also included a worn recliner, a tacky coffee table made from a wagon wheel, a footstool covered in cowskin, and an old rolltop desk. Only the computer on the battered rolltop desk escaped the dirt, shrouded as it was with a plastic cover.

If she just stood absolutely still for a few days, the dust would probably begin to collect on her, too. Grabbing a towel and the flannel shirt, she set off in search of soap and water. The kitchen wasn't hard to find seeing as how there were only three rooms in the entire house—Travis's bedroom, the living room and the room she stood in now.

A huge plank table with benches on either side sat in the middle of the kitchen. Two of the four walls were lined with utilitarian cabinets and appliances—a commercial refrigerator, a chest freezer, a restaurant-style stove with a griddle, a washing machine and dryer, and even a water heater—all of them chipped and scarred and dented from years of hard use. The room didn't even come close to cozy—or charming.

She gave only a cursory glance to the door on the back wall that lead to the loathsome outhouse. She'd be damned if she was about to step outside the relative safety of the house while it was still dark. If she had to go, she'd just have to wait until morning. No civilized person could be expected to leave the house in the middle of the night to use the bathroom.

Shrugging out of Travis's coat, she stepped up to the sink and flipped on the faucets. The tiara came off first and then the pins that held her long braids in place. She worked her fingers through her hair until it lay loose around her shoulders, nearly reaching her waist. Next, she slowly stripped off her costume, letting the gown pool on the floor at her feet. As she sank her bare arms into the warm water, she sighed. If ever she truly needed a hot bubble bath, it was now. But a sinkful of soapy water was all she had to wash the dust from her skin and send the chill from her bones.

When she finished washing, she slipped out of her torn tights and tossed them in the trash, then took off her bra and panties and washed them in the soapy water. She looped them through a towel ring. Wrapped in the flannel shirt, she padded back to the couch to make up her bed. The living room was as cold as the kitchen and she quickly crawled between the two wool blankets.

Where had she gotten the idea that Arizona was supposed to be warm? Josie closed her eyes and pulled the blanket up under her nose. But a half hour later she still hadn't dozed off. The couch was lumpy, the blankets itched, and the pillow wasn't down-filled. The chili was eating its way through her stomach. The kitchen sink dripped, she was freezing . . . and she had to go to the bathroom.

With a silent curse Josie threw back the blanket and crawled off the couch. An hour ago the thirty-yard trip to the outhouse, armed with a flashlight and rifle, had been an unthinkable option. But with at least five hours to go until dawn, Josie knew she'd have to make the trip sooner or later. Either that, or spend the rest of the evening pacing around the living room.

She wandered back into the kitchen and peeked out the window. A low howl sounded in the distance and she jumped away from the door. The rifle was propped in the corner, the flashlight on the floor beside it. She tried to imagine defending herself against a wild animal with that gun, but she'd never held a gun in her life. Nor could she recall ever seeing a real wild animal.

And then she realized that she wouldn't have to. This may not be the Plaza, but Travis McKinnon had to make at least a few concessions to his houseguest. She wasn't about to go to the outhouse alone!

She hurried through the kitchen and living room to Travis's bedroom door and pushed it open. The room was dimly lit, a stream of light from the closet illuminating the body sprawled across the bed.

"McKinnon?" she whispered.

He didn't move. Not a tremble or a twitch.

"McKinnon," she said, this time in a normal tone.

Even this didn't bring as much as a blink or a snort. The man slept like a tenant at the local mortuary.

"Travis McKinnon!" she shouted. "Wake up! I have to go to the outhouse and you're going to take me!" She stepped up to the bed and poked him on the shoulder.

If she hadn't heard his soft, even breathing, she would have wondered if he'd passed on to the great rodeo in the sky. He was still dressed in his shirt and jeans, though he'd managed to pull off his boots before he'd tumbled onto the bed.

Josie watched him for a long moment, holding her breath and remaining absolutely still. Every instinct told her to shake him again, to wake him up and demand an escort to the outhouse. But she couldn't. She stood silently over him, mesmerized by the man in front of her.

He looked so vulnerable, like a little boy, with his hair all mussed up and his face smooth and untroubled. The deep tan of his face was marred only by tiny crow's-feet in a paler shade radiating from the corners of his eyes out to his striking cheekbones. His wide mouth was curved up slightly as if he enjoyed a pleasant dream.

Her gaze moved to his hand, resting on the pillow beside his head. She slowly knelt down beside the bed and stared at his open palm. A little boy inside a man, a man who worked hard during the day and slept just as hard at night. Her finger traced the deep calluses that marked the flesh at the base of each finger and she winced inwardly as she encountered a jagged cut, barely healed.

He wasn't quite like the cowboys at Javelina's, though she wasn't sure why. Maybe it was here, in his long, straight fingers, so different from the gnarled, overworked hands of Harley and the others.

But there was something more. Even in slumber, dressed in a flannel shirt and torn jeans, Travis McKinnon possessed something none of those other cowboys had. An inbred resolve, a confidence that seemed to project from his every movement, from the angle of his jaw to the swagger in his step. If it didn't seem so outrageous, she'd have to call it . . . sophistication.

Her hand shook slightly as she pulled it away. She slowly stood and backed toward the closet, then turned to push the door open a few more inches, allowing a bit more light to spill into the room and onto his handsome face. But as she turned back to Travis, she realized that the light coming from the closet wasn't really coming from a closet at all.

It came from . . . a bathroom! Josie stifled a cry of delight. A glorious indoor bathroom with a toilet and a double vanity and glass block shower stall and a roomy whirlpool tub! She slipped inside and quietly closed the door. The wide mirror reflected her smile as she took in all that the room had to offer. Unlike the rest of the house, the bathroom was new and modern and perfectly spotless. Exactly like the bathrooms at . . . the Plaza.

Josie ground her teeth and cursed Travis Mc-Kinnon's sick sense of humor. The creep! He was sending *her* to the outhouse while *he* had a perfectly fine *indoor* bathroom for himself. Well, it would serve him right if she *had* attempted a trip outside and had gotten eaten by a hungry coyote on the way. He would have been sorry then. Why, it would almost be considered murder, and all in the name of protecting his precious indoor plumbing!

Josie turned on the shower and unbuttoned the plaid flannel shirt. If he was determined to make her life miserable, then she would return the favor, for as long as she resided at Castle Creek Ranch.

But first, she'd take a shower. A long, hot, bone-deep shower, guaranteed to wash away any kindhearted thoughts she might have harbored about the black-hearted cowboy asleep in the next room.

THE SOUND of running water teased at his mind, drawing him out of the depths of sleep into consciousness. Rain, Travis thought, smiling sleepily. He never realized how much of his life would come to depend on that sound. Everything in the desert seemed to turn on a simple act of nature, an event that was merely an annoyance back in Chicago.

Travis listened, his eyes still closed, letting the soothing sound wash over him. Maybe he could afford to sleep in today. His exhaustion had barely been sated; he felt even more tired than he had when he'd crawled into bed. But rain or no rain, the transmission had to be replaced on the northeast windmill. He and the boys had to drive the cattle up to that pasture within the next few days for fresh grazing and they couldn't do that unless there was water waiting.

His blurry mind gradually began to spin with all the chores he had ahead of him. The fence in the west pasture had to be fixed, and before long they'd have to bring in the remuda, the extra horses that had been put out to pasture in the fall after the busy work was done.

And then, it would start all over again. Spring gathering began in mid-February and the work didn't end until the following fall. Herding, culling, branding, and then, in midsummer, turning the cattle back out to graze. There was a pleasing rhythm to it all, as if nature and man moved as one, each taking its cues from the other.

Travis focused on the rain again, trying to empty his mind for just a little longer. But something about the sound nagged at his mind. The corrugated tin roof usually amplified the noise of the rain until a gentle sprinkle nearly rattled the foundations of the ranch house. Suddenly the sound stopped, as if Mother Nature had shut off a faucet. And then he realized he hadn't been listening to the rain, he'd been listening to his shower.

In that instant all the events of the previous evening paraded back into his brain and at the head of the line was Princess Josephine. Travis groaned and threw his arm over his eyes. With all the problems he had to deal with on Castle Creek, why did she pick now to pay a royal visit? If her mere presence wasn't bad enough, he now had a damned naked woman in his shower. It seemed as if his luck was only getting worse.

The door to the bathroom opened and Travis turned his head slightly, his arm still shadowing his eyes. She paused before stepping out and he slowed his breathing. She tiptoed across the room toward the door and he shifted his arm to afford a better view. At the faint sound of his movement, she froze, caught halfway to the door, her profile visible in the light from the bathroom.

He was tempted to speak, but instead he just watched her. God, she looked sexy standing in the middle of his bedroom in nothing but his flannel shirt. The shirt nearly reached her knees, but there was enough leg showing along the open shirttail to tantalize his senses. Her damp hair tumbled over her shoulders to her lower back, loose and much longer than he'd imagined.

She took a tentative step and he shifted again, rustling the sheets with his foot. He smiled. If he played his cards right, he could probably keep her in his bedroom all night, making a move every time she inched her way to the door.

A vision of her standing nude in his shower, water sluicing over her slender body, flashed in his mind and he felt himself growing hard as he lost himself in the fantasy. He'd open the shower door and step inside, pulling her soap-slicked body into his arms and running his hands over her skin. She'd wind her arms around his neck, hot and ready for him, whispering her desire. And then, when he couldn't stand it any longer, he'd—

Travis ground his teeth and squeezed his eyes shut, trying to will his mutinous reaction away. She took another step and the floor squeaked, but this time Travis decided to let her go. She may be great fantasy material, but Princess Josephine would be gone in less than twenty-four hours. And he had more than enough ranch work to occupy his mind—and his body.

Besides, he had to face the facts. There wasn't a woman in the world who would choose to live on Castle Creek. His former fiancée, a woman who had professed to love him, had lasted only three weeks before the dust and the isolation and the endless days alone had finally sent her packing. And considering Princess Josephine's aversion to wildlife and insects, the lack of plumbing, and not to mention *him*, she probably wouldn't last a week.

No, Princess Josephine was definitely a high-maintenance, city-bred, spoiled-rotten woman. Not the kind of woman a man could depend on to share in the running of a working ranch. Still, there were the long, lonely nights to consider. And a beautiful woman like the princess would be a warm addition to his cold bed.

For the next twenty minutes he tried to sleep. Then, with a silent curse, Travis rolled off the bed and stumbled to his feet. There was no way he was going to get any sleep with her in the other room, her sweet little body clothed in his favorite flannel shirt. He grabbed his boots from the floor and flung open his bedroom door, then strode through the living room.

Josephine pushed up from the couch and blinked sleepily, her gaze following him across the room. "Where are you going? Is something wrong? I heard an animal howling before. Do you think it's the coyotes?"

"I've got work to do," he muttered. "Where's my jacket?" Travis headed toward the kitchen. He found his jacket in a heap on the floor, underneath her gown. In addition, he found her underwear hanging from the towel rack. Travis touched the silky fabric and another unbidden image of her naked body appeared in his mind.

With a hiss of frustration, he headed back to the living room to collect his hat.

"Do you realize it's three o'clock in the morning?" she asked, brushing her rumpled hair from her eyes. "It's still dark out. How are you going to work in the dark?"

Travis stared down at her. No, Princess Josephine probably wouldn't last a week on Castle Creek. She was too beautiful, too delicate, to spend her life in the desert. But he was not going to take the time to find out for sure.

"I've got things to do," Travis snapped. "Besides, as soon as the sun comes up I'm taking you back to Tucson, Princess. Make sure you're ready."

# 3

THE SMELL of freshly brewed coffee wafted through the ranch house and teased at Josie's nose. She stretched her arms over her head and lazily opened her eyes. Early morning sunshine angled through the dingy multi-paned windows and dust motes danced on the shafts of soft golden light, but the sun did little to warm the chilly room.

Josie pulled the blanket up to her nose and smiled contentedly. This was the first morning of her new life and already it was everything she'd dreamed of. Richie wasn't pounding on her hotel room door, screaming at her that the bus was ready to leave. David wasn't railing at her for being late to rehearsal for the fifth time in a week. And Misha wasn't telling her to point her toe or tuck in her elbow or arch her back or smile, smile, smile. In fact, if she didn't want to, she'd never have to smile again.

Josie levered herself up and dragged the blanket around her shoulders. That life was in the past now, and she wasn't about to spend her first morning lounging around on a lumpy couch and reliving former figure-skating exploits. She had places to go and things to do, though exactly what they were she wasn't quite sure. But Travis McKinnon had vowed to return her to Tucson as soon as the sun came up, and by her reckoning, it was well past dawn.

As a child she'd always risen in the dark, pulling on her clothes with her eyes half shut, dozing off as Edmund, the family chauffeur, drove her to the rink. Four hours later her mother would pick her up and, after a long progress report from her coach, she would hurry Josie off to classes at an exclusive private school. Josie had always dreaded that part of the morning, trapped in the car with Evelyn, subjected to a review of all her flaws and mistakes and inconsistencies.

Even as an adult, she felt a wave of trepidation every time she opened a car door. Her defenses automatically went on alert and her mind sharpened to stay a step ahead of whatever accusations her mother threw at her. Misha had been right. Her behavior had become just a way to protect herself, to hide her insecurities and insulate her fears.

Yawning, she brushed her tangled hair over her shoulder. Well, she was in charge of her own life now. At least there would be no one around to tell her what a mess she was making of it. As far as Travis McKinnon was concerned, she was a runaway princess, not Josephine Eastman, fractious figure skater.

Josie rubbed her neck, trying to work the kinks out of her stiff body. Sometime in the wee hours before dawn, the couch had managed to pummel her into a mass of aching muscles and creaking joints. But even if she'd had twenty feather mattresses stacked one on top of the other, she still would have gone sleepless. Though Travis McKinnon wasn't exactly the pea that had kept the princess awake in the famous fairy tale, thoughts of him had still managed to keep her from sleeping for most of the night.

A woman like herself—any woman, for that matter—could spend too many sleepless hours fantasizing about the sexy cowboy sprawled across the bed in the adjoining room...about his rugged good looks and his devilish smile, about his hard, muscular chest and strong, sinewy arms. About his long legs and his tight butt and how he'd feel on top of her, or underneath her, or inside—

"Breakfast's on." The gravely voice came out of nowhere, splitting the silence and startling all traces of Travis from her mind. Josie turned to find a strange man standing just beyond the end of the couch, watching her with a penetrating one-eyed stare from beneath the brim of his black cowboy hat. With a scream of alarm, she scrambled to her feet and retreated to the far side of the coffee table.

How long had he been watching her? A few seconds? A few hours? She certainly hadn't heard him enter the room, though considering the subject of her brief lapse into lusting, a jet plane could have landed in the living room without her hearing it. She tried to recall whether any embarrassing noises—a sigh, or maybe a moan—had accompanied her daydream, but all she had left of the fantasy was a racing pulse and a warm tingle in the vicinity of her—Josie drew a steadying breath.

"Who are you?" she demanded. "Where's Travis?"

She swallowed hard as her gaze took in his black eye patch and his craggy, sun-lined face, his whip-thin body and that one pale, unblinking eye. The cowboy stared at her like she was some strange new species looking up at him through the wrong end of a microscope. He couldn't have been much more than two or three inches taller than her five-foot-four-inch height, but he looked disproportionately surly for his size. His age was as much a mystery as his identity, somewhere between sixty and the grave. One thing was clear—this man wasn't here with the Deadwater Gulch Welcoming Committee.

"Who *are* you?" she repeated. An icy edge crept into her voice, a weapon she used whenever she felt threatened or uncertain. Like whenever a one-eyed man was staring a hole through her forehead.

"Snake," the man stated.

Josie screeched and jumped up on the couch. "Where?" she cried, scanning the floor. She glanced over at the man for help, but he stood, unmoving and unafraid, stuck in the same spot like a cigar store Indian. Though his expression remained stoic, she caught a smile quirking one corner of his mouth.

"You mean, your *name* is Snake?" she asked, already realizing her mistake. He refused to reply. Well, what did he expect her to think? Snake might be a perfectly common name for a cowboy, but she didn't know many figure skaters who were named after poisonous reptiles. Upon further thought, the name seemed appropriate considering the man's appearance.

"Well, Mr. . . . Snake, I'd appreciate it if you'd stop staring at me like that and tell me where Travis is."

"Gone." He nodded, as if dead certain of that answer.

Though she'd known Mr. Snake less than a minute, he had an irritating knack for stating the obvious, and doing so with a minimum of words. "Where?" she asked climbing off the couch. "He promised to take me back to Tucson as soon as the sun was up."

He shrugged. "Breakfast's on," he said, crossing the room to the kitchen in a rocking, bow-legged gait.

Josie watched him through narrowed eyes, fighting back a surge of temper at his casual dismissal. "Wait just a minute, Mr. Snake," she called, tossing the blanket down and stalking after him. "I asked you a question and I want you to—" She stopped dead as she entered the kitchen. Newt and Harley looked up from their plates, Harley with an appreciative grin and Newt with his mouth agape.

"Mornin', Yer Highness," Harley said.

"Yer—yer lookin' mighty purdy this mornin', Princess," Newt choked out through a mouthful of food.

A flash of embarrassment shot through her. Though Travis's flannel shirt covered much more than most of her skating costumes, Harley and Newt seemed particularly fascinated with her bare legs and feet. She tugged at the tail of her shirt, hoping it covered her naked backside. But that only pulled the front up along her thighs, causing Newt to drop his fork and Harley to clear his throat.

Tearing his eyes away from the sight, Newt pushed up from the table, knocking over his glass of milk on the way. He nearly fell over backward trying to crawl over the bench. At first Josie thought she'd frightened him, but then she saw what he was after. Newt grabbed her tiara from the kitchen counter and held it out to her with nervous hands.

Josie took the tiara and placed it on top of her head. That brought a look to Newt's cherubic face she'd only observed before on puppies in a pet store window. The kind of expression that said, "Take me home and I'll promise to love you." Well, at least he wasn't panting and drooling.

Glancing away from the boy's moony-eyed gaze, Josie noticed the array of food laid out on the kitchen table. Her stomach growled and her mouth watered. "Could that be eggs Benedict you're eating?" she asked.

Harley looked down at his plate and frowned. "This here's a poached cackleberry settin' on a slab of sow butt and a doughgod, with yeller sauce over it. It's one of Snake's specialties. Ain't that right, Snake?"

Snake didn't bother to reply. He placed another plate on the table and nodded in her direction, a silent invitation to sit down. Josie didn't wait to be asked again. She slipped onto the bench.

Newt scrambled to sit down beside her. This *was* eggs Benedict, Western style, with the most incredible Hollandaise sauce she'd ever tasted. The buttermilk biscuit was warm and flaky, and the ham had to be imported. Imagine, eggs Benedict in the middle of nowhere.

"You made this?" she asked, looking up at Snake.

Snake didn't reply. Instead he turned his attention back to the stove.

"Snake does all the cookin' at Castle Creek," Harley said. "He's been workin' here long as anyone can remember. Snake started working for Travis's granddaddy back when Travis's daddy was no more than a button. Ain't that right, Snake?"

Again, Snake didn't reply. At least she wasn't the only person who rendered Snake mute. In fact, Josie wondered whether "Ain't that right, Snake?" was just the cowboys' way of including their silent friend in the conversation.

"Snake taught Travis to ride," Harley said. "Travis first come here when he was just a boy and he was scared of horses. Snake says he couldn't find his saddle seat with a forked stick." Harley chuckled. "Every time he got on a horse, he kissed the ground, ain't that right, Snake? Well, Snake took the boy in hand and tied him onto that saddle and slapped that horse in his ass and—"

"You cain't say 'ass' in front of the princess, Harley," Newt whispered. "It ain't proper."

Harley rolled his eyes. "All right, his git-up end. You satisfied?"

Newt nodded.

"That horse burned the breeze all the way out to the north pasture," Harley continued. "When Travis rode back, he was grinning like a hinny in a haybarn. His ass—"

Newt jabbed Harley in the side with his elbow. Harley gave Newt a shove and a warning look before he went on.

"I mean, Travis's git-up end was sore for a month of Sundays. But he crawled off that horse and told Snake he wanted to be a cowboy when he grew up. He come back here every summer since then," Harley concluded. "Until he started working for his daddy, that is."

"Thanks to Snake," Newt added, "Travis is wild, woolly and full o' fleas."

"Fleas?" Josie asked. In addition to coyotes, mountain lions, and scorpions, now she'd have to worry about fleas? She scratched her arm distractedly and wondered when those wool blankets had last seen the dry cleaners. The couch could be a veritable flea condo for all she knew.

"That just means he's a good man," Newt said. "He ain't no citified knothead."

"You mean, Travis wasn't born here?" Josie asked.

"No, ma'am," Newt said. "He was born up near Chicago. Travis's daddy got enough money to burn a wet mule. He weren't too pleased when Travis moved down here last year after Smilin' Jack died."

"What did he—" Josie's next question was interrupted by Snake. He didn't speak, just cleared his throat, but that was all it took for Newt and Harley to push away from the table and grab their hats.

"We got to be gettin' to work now, Yer Highness," Harley said. "You have a nice day, now."

Newt blushed and tipped his hat. "'Bye, ma'am."

The boys loped to the door and walked outside, leaving Josie alone with Snake, the Wild West's most brilliant conversationalist. As she slowly finished her breakfast, Snake cleared the table and washed the dishes. He went about his work as if she wasn't even there, never glancing her way, never acknowledging her existence. The man was a complete mystery and, the truth be told, more than a little intimidating. She'd certainly be glad when Travis returned to take her back to Tucson.

Josie took a sip of her coffee. The warm brew was rich and strong, exactly the way she liked it. What talents Snake lacked in interpersonal communications, he more than made up for in the kitchen.

"Do you know when Travis will be back?" she asked. "And do you think you might be able to give me more than a one-word answer on this one?"

He turned to Josie, his direct gaze intimating that he didn't appreciate her commentary. "Nope," he answered, wiping his hands on a dish towel.

"Do you know where he is?"

"Nope." Snake frowned, then pulled the dish towel from the towel ring and examined it closely. A look of shock suffused his stoic expression and he glanced up at Josie. Slowly he walked across the kitchen and dropped the wadded towel next to her plate. "Yours," he said.

The underwear she'd washed in the kitchen sink the night before now sat beside the remains of her eggs Benedict. She glanced up, but Snake was gone. Scared off by a pair of bikini panties and a lacy bra. She stuffed the underwear into the pocket of her shirt and grabbed her coffee mug. At least she knew what to do the next time Snake stared at her. She'd just wave some ladies' lingerie under his nose and watch him turn tail and run.

Josie plucked another biscuit from the plate on the table and wandered into the living room. Already the house was warming up under the early morning sun. She wrapped the blanket around her, then opened the front door and peered out at the yard. No slathering coyotes or snarling mountain lions. Not even a scorpion to be seen. Nor was there any sign of Travis McKinnon.

As she stepped out onto the porch, Josie's breath stopped in her throat. She blinked hard. A strange, desolate land spread out before her, stretching from the porch to the horizon, wide and open with no sign of civilization in sight. The rising sun hovered over a distant mountain range, bathing the desert in shimmering light. Nothing seemed familiar, not the trees, not the land, not even the sky.

The house was like a tiny island adrift in the midst of nothingness. Two gnarled, stunted trees stood sentinel by the house, but beyond the yard, the ground was dry and dusty and broken only by small clumps of colorless brush. Even the weathered sheds seemed to fade into the rolling landscape.

Still, in all the desolation, there was an overwhelming solitude, a frightening power that seemed to hold her in its grip, as if she were the only person on earth.

A person could be alone here like no other place on earth.

She sat down in an old rocker and clutched her coffee mug in stiff fingers, her gaze still fixed on the blue-gray mountain range that split the horizon. A wave of anxiety washed over her. She didn't belong here, out in the middle of nowhere with civilization miles away. People didn't live on land like this, they survived. And though Josie considered herself a survivor, even she couldn't imagine life in this vast wasteland.

Her fantasy life included shopping malls and fine restaurants, movie theaters and take-out pizza, luxury hotels and noisy nightclubs. From what she saw last night of Deadwater Gulch, neither Bloomingdale's nor the Plaza would be opening a branch there anytime soon.

She definitely needed to get back to civilization. Her plan for a new life did not include a run-down ranch and its accompanying cowboy. Besides, she sensed a real danger in her attraction toward Travis, as if she hovered on the edge of a steep precipice. This was a man who could probably wield an incredible power over a woman, a man who could hold both her mind and her body hostage.

The sooner she left Travis McKinnon behind, the better.

DAYLIGHT was nearly gone by the time Travis pulled up in front of the ranch house. He had spent the past twelve hours trying to install the new transmission on the windmill in the northeast pasture, but the blasted thing refused to line up.

At first he was determined to fix the windmill, no matter how long it took him. But when desert darkness began it set in, he realized that he really didn't give a damn about the windmill. On a normal day he would have thrown in the towel after just two hours. The truth be told, he didn't want to set foot inside the ranch house.

Though he didn't know the princess well, he knew that she was anxious to get back to Tucson. He'd broken his word and the last thing he needed was a royal tongue-lashing. But he'd told her that he would take her back in the morning. And he had intended to do just that—until he'd had to spend an entire day on a one-hour job.

Travis hopped out of the truck and waved at Snake who was sitting on the front porch of the bunkhouse. Usually, Snake could be found in the kitchen at sunset, putting the final touches on another one of his gastronomic masterpieces. One of the county's best calf ropers, Snake had hung up his lariat a few years back and taken over the cooking chores at Castle Creek.

At first Snake had prepared classic ranch fare— beans, biscuits and beef. But then Harley had given him a Julia Child cookbook for his birthday. The cookbook had been meant as a joke, but Snake had taken it seriously and immediately set to learning the intricacies of French cooking. Suddenly, Snake's greatest dream had changed from dying with his boots on to living long enough to meet Julia Child and study at the Cordon Bleu. But until he mastered the French language and saved enough for a plane ticket to Paris, he had agreed to serve as Castle Creek's "chef" and Travis's business advisor.

Snake knew Castle Creek better than anyone—alive or dead. Smilin' Jack McKinnon was a terrific grandfather, and an even better cowboy. But his own breed-in' bull had a better sense for business than Smilin' Jack. Snake was the only reason there was a Castle Creek left for Travis to inherit. So, in a way, Snake was entitled to more than just a warm corner and a soft bed.

Travis strolled over to the bunkhouse and sat down on the porch step next to Snake. "The fitting on that transmission doesn't line up. I'm going to have to take it back into Tucson tomorrow and have Ed machine it down."

Snake nodded, continuing to whittle a piece of mountain ash into a perfect replica of a horse. Snake's horses were sold at a gift shop in Bisbee and had earned him a tidy little nest egg for his retirement.

"Is she mad?" Travis asked.

"Yep," Snake said.

"Is that why you're out here and not in the kitchen?"

"Yep."

"The boys'll be comin' in soon," Travis said. "They're going to want to eat."

"I ain't goin' back in there," Snake said. "Last time I opened the door, she lit into me like a swarm of heel flies."

"Don't tell me you're scared of her," Travis said with a chuckle.

"Just get her out of that house and out of my kitchen, or you and the boys'll be eatin' cut straw and molasses for a week."

Travis pushed up to his feet. "I'm takin' her back to Tucson tomorrow morning along with that bad transmission. And don't worry. If you promise to bake a boggy-top cherry pie for dessert, I'll promise to get her out of the house for a while."

Snake nodded. "Done."

Travis strode toward the house. With all the work he had to complete before turning in, he'd find something for the princess to do. Maybe there was a ship she could christen or a few babies she could kiss. Or maybe he could find her something dirty and smelly to do. Something that might convince her to take another midnight shower in his bathroom.

The kitchen door swung open before he could grab the knob. She stood in the doorway, dressed in his favorite flannel shirt and a pair of his jeans. Her feet were still bare, but she had braided her hair. Her little diamond crown was nowhere to be seen.

"It's about time you got back. Where have you been?"

"Hey there, Tinker Bell." He pushed past her and headed toward the refrigerator. She followed, hot on his heels.

"I've been waiting for you all day. You promised you'd take me back to Tucson, or did you forget?"

"How could I forget you, Tink?" he teased. He had to admit that she looked even more beautiful when she was in a high temper, full of spit and fire, her green eyes blazing, her face flushed. This was no milquetoast miss. This was a woman who was used to getting exactly what she wanted. And right now, she wanted his head on a platter.

"Where were you?" she demanded. "I want to leave. Now! I have important things to take care of."

"And I have work to do," Travis said. He grabbed a beer from the refrigerator and popped the top, then took a long drink. Wiping his hand across his mouth, he stifled a burp, then gave her a grin. "Us common folk have to do that now and then. And if you want a place to sleep tonight, you're going to help me."

"Help you? I'm your guest. I'm not going to work. Besides, I'm not staying here tonight. You're taking me back."

He grabbed her hand and pulled her along with him into the living room. "See those boots?" He pointed to the pair gathering dust on the living room rug. "Put 'em on."

She glared at him, folding her arms across her chest. "No."

"Put them on, Tink, or you don't eat tonight."

She snatched the boots from the floor and tugged them on her feet. "Just because I'm doing this," she grumbled, "does not mean you can boss me around. If everyone else on the ranch works for their meals, then so will I. Just for tonight, of course."

"Of course," Travis said. From her easy compliance, he suspected that she'd already enjoyed at least one of Snake's meals and didn't want to miss another.

"And you can stop calling me Tink," she muttered. "My name is Josephine."

Travis raised a brow. "Is it? Or is that just a part of your princess story."

"It's not a story," she said, clumping across the wood floor.

He opened the front door for her and swept his hand out in a courtly gesture. "Your subjects await," he said.

"What subjects?"

"Well, I thought we'd start with the chicken coop. Then I thought you could give my horse a bath. And after that, I thought I'd have you milk Winnie."

"Who's Winnie? A cow?"

"Your traveling companion from last night."

"Oh, no," Josie said. "I'm not going near that goat."

Travis laughed. "Knowing you, I don't expect you'll get past the chicken coop."

"What is that supposed to mean?"

"Well, out here on Castle Creek we don't have much use for a well-trained princess. But we can always use an extra hand to muck out the chicken coop." Travis placed a small pitchfork in a rusty wheelbarrow, then pointed to a small shed with an attached wire pen. "Go inside the shed, gather up all the dirty straw and put it in the wheelbarrow. Then lay down some fresh bedding. After you're done, I want you to chase those chickens into their little house so the coatis don't get 'em."

She glanced around the pen warily. "What's a coati? Is it poisonous?"

"Coatimundi. It's like a ring-tail possum, or a raccoon. They have a particular taste for poultry."

"Finally," Josie muttered. "An animal that doesn't prefer people for dinner."

"Do you think you can handle the job?"

"I'm not an idiot," she said.

"No, I don't suppose you are," he replied.

But by the time she finished with the chicken coop, Travis was certain she *would* feel like an idiot. It took her four tries before she managed to maneuver the wheelbarrow through the narrow pen door. She warily entered the shed. A moment later, she reappeared, waving her hand in front of her nose.

"Yee-ow! I don't know why I'm worried about the coyotes. The smell of that shed is enough to kill me."

"Don't worry, Princess. A little chicken poop never hurt anyone."

She pinched her nose and stepped back inside. Travis turned to busy himself with polishing his saddle, tossed over the nearby hitching rail. But watching Josie was much more fun and he found his attention drawn again and again to the chicken coop.

Ten minutes later she emerged with a wheelbarrow full of dirty straw. Getting the full wheelbarrow out of the pen was even harder than the trip in. She managed to tip it over three times. The second time, as she fought off the advances of a rather nasty hen, she stumbled backward over the pitchfork and fell on her backside right on top of the pile.

To his surprise, she quickly picked herself up, wiped her hands on her jeans, and tried again. Travis smiled. She was a determined little princess, he had to give her that.

Though she gamely cleaned out the coop, chicken herding wasn't a skill she'd learned in princess training school. The rest of the flock took their cues from the aggressive hen and flew at her whenever she attempted to shoo them from the pen into the shed. The birds spent more time chasing her than she spent chasing them. Travis wove his fingers through the chicken wire, stifling a chuckle, and watched her for a few minutes more before he decided to put an end to the performance.

"These chickens do not want to go inside their house," she grumbled.

He opened the wire door and handed her a bucket of cracked corn. "Here, try this. Take this feed inside the shed and dump it in the trays."

With a dubious look, she grabbed the bucket from him and did as she was told. She reappeared in the doorway of the shed and he opened the pen, motioning her outside. They stood and watched as, one by one, the chickens headed into the shed. She blinked in disbelief. "It worked. Look at that. They're going inside."

Travis didn't bother to tell her that chickens always headed back inside the shed at sunset to roost—with or without food. "Go close the door before they get out again," he instructed.

Once she had secured the shed door, Travis opened the pen and ushered her out. "Nice job," he said, plucking a piece of straw from her hair. "I think you might just have a way with chickens."

"Really?" she asked. A soft vulnerable look crossed her features, as if she suddenly needed his approval.

Travis couldn't find it in himself to tell her he was being sarcastic. He took the bucket from her hand and grinned. "Really."

Princess Josephine glanced up at him with a smile, warm and radiant, like the first rays of sun breaking across the desert on a crisp winter morning. He'd been so long without a woman, he'd forgotten the kind of effect a simple, feminine smile could have on him. He turned his face toward the warmth.

At that moment she looked incredibly alluring. Wisps of dark hair curled around her flushed face and bits of straw clung to the long braid that hung over her shoulder. The heavy makeup she had worn the previous night had been washed away, revealing skin so smooth it begged to be touched. He wanted to place his palm on her cheek and let that silky warmth seep into him. He gripped the bucket with a white-knuckled hand instead.

"Come on, Tink," he ordered. "Let's see how you do with horses."

She hitched up her jeans, then clomped after him, her oversize boots sending clouds of dust around her feet. "I wish you wouldn't call me Tink. I hate that name."

"What would you like me to call you? Princess doesn't seem to fit now that you're dressed like a common cowgirl."

"You can call me Josie," she said.

Travis stopped and looked down at her. The princess facade was gone and somehow he knew he was seeing the real woman behind the fabrications. "Josie?"

She nodded. "Short for Josephine. It's what my friends call me."

"Am I your friend?" Travis asked.

She stared at the toe of her boot, tracing a pattern in the dust. "You're an acquaintance. But it's silly for you to call me Princess. I don't feel or look much like a princess right now."

"And you don't smell much like one, either," Travis added.

She glared at him.

"I'm sorry about that," Travis said. "But it comes with the job."

"Don't be sorry," Josie conceded. "I really don't mind. Most times I'd just like to forget I'm a princess anyway."

Travis grabbed a halter and lead rope from the gate post, then opened the the corral and stepped inside. Castle Creek's corral was a hodgepodge circular structure made of shoulder-high stout branches and old boards lashed together with baling wire and rawhide and twine and anything else that happened to be handy. The gate was store-bought, though, reinforced steel piping that swung easily on its hinges.

During the busy season, the corral held almost thirty horses. Each hand at Castle Creek had a string of five horses and Snake kept two for his occasional use. The rest were ridden by the seasonal help. But during the fall and winter, Travis and the hands kept only two horses. The rest of the remuda roamed the range, taking a well-deserved break from the cutting and trailing and roping that occupied the balance of the year.

Josie climbed up on the gate and watched him as he slipped the halter over the horse's head and clipped on the lead. But as he approached the gate, the horse at his side, her eyes widened. Travis's horse was a solid, sixteen-hand, chestnut quarter horse, sixty-four inches from the ground to the base of his mane, an animal that had more cow sense than any other horse on Castle Creek.

And Josie was a petite sixteen-hand princess who looked positively tiny next to his horse. But the chestnut was an even-tempered gelding who took particular delight in nipping at Travis's shirt pocket in search of his favorite peppermints. It took more than a woman to rattle this horse. If Josie just stayed out from under his feet, she'd be fine.

"I'm supposed to give *that* a bath?" she asked, scrambling off the gate.

Travis led the horse out and handed her the lead rope. "Take him over there by that hitching rail. I'll go get the brushes and combs you'll need."

He was halfway to the tack shed when she called out to him. "What's his name?" she asked.

Travis turned. "He doesn't really have a name," he replied. "Sometimes I call him Red. Mostly I call him Horse."

"Red," she repeated. "That's sort of an ordinary name. I thought cowboys called their horses Trigger or Silver or Buttercup."

"He's just an ordinary horse. He's not a movie star. Besides, most cowboys would tell you not to name an animal you might have to eat in a pinch."

She crinkled her nose in disgust. "I guess I'll have to pay closer attention to what Snake puts on my plate."

A few minutes later Travis returned with two buckets, one filled with old grooming tools and the other with water. He couldn't remember the last time a horse had been groomed at Castle Creek. Smilin' Jack had kept a couple of Arabians and had enjoyed spit-polishing them until they'd shone, but Travis had sold the pair the month after he'd arrived. Though Arabians made decent cow ponies, his grandfather's coddling and the horses' high-spirited temperaments had made them ill-suited for ranch work. Besides, he'd needed the extra money.

Josie stood where he'd left her, regarding Red warily from the other end of the lead rope. She covered her nose with her hand. "When was the last time this horse was bathed? He smells worse than those chickens."

Travis laughed at the haughty tone in her voice. She spoke as if he'd somehow been deficient in the care of his mount. "He's never had a bath in his life that I can recall." None of the Castle Creek stock had, at least not since Travis was ten years old.

She frowned. "Then why am *I* washing him now?"

"Don't you think it's about time? Take this rag and scrub down his coat. When you run out of water, fill the bucket from the water trough inside the corral. After you've rubbed down his coat, brush him and curry his mane and tail. You can tie him to that hitching post over there while you work. And keep your toes out from under his feet. And don't let him kick you. Or bite you."

"Is there anything that doesn't bite on this ranch?" Josie asked.

Travis grinned. "I don't." Satisfied that he'd given her all the instructions she needed, he strolled across the yard, sat down in the rocker on the porch and kicked his feet up on the railing.

Josie stood in the middle of the yard, buckets at her feet, the lead rope still clutched in her right hand. "Aren't you going to help me?" she shouted.

Travis wove his fingers together behind his head and leaned back. "I'm the big sugar, Tink. The boss man. I own this ranch and I don't have to help if I don't want to. Besides, I'd rather watch."

And watch he did. She bent over and dipped the rag in the bucket, presenting him with a perfect view of her backside. Travis stifled a moan. Even in the oversize clothes, she was pretty damn cute. But he couldn't help but wish for a pair of jeans that fit her properly. Travis pulled his hat down low and watched her through narrowed eyes. Yeah, he'd definitely trade his kingdom for a pair of smaller jeans.

Travis thought she was doing quite well, considering the size of the beast she was bathing, though she seemed to be getting more water on herself than on the horse. He closed his eyes and smiled.

Suddenly a scream pierced the air. Travis pulled his hat off and shot to his feet. He was ready to fetch the shotgun until he heard her shout.

"Get off my foot, you stupid beast!" Josie stood near Red's rump, beating the horse with the backside of the dandy brush. Red glanced back at her and watched her lazily, then indolently shook himself from head to tail, showering her with more water. This caused another round of vicious threats to Red's life, including one that involved a one-way ticket to the glue factory.

The horse had the toe of Josie's boot trapped under his foot and he wasn't about to move. She pushed against him with her shoulder, but she was no match for the half-ton horse.

Travis ran across the yard. "I told you to watch out for his feet," he said, shoving against the horse's side. Red sidestepped off Josie's foot and she groaned in relief. "Are you all right?"

"He could have broken my foot!" she cried. "My right foot! Do you know what a broken right foot would mean to my career? That's the foot I pick with, the foot I—" She stopped short, then turned away, as if she'd revealed too much. "Never mind," she said softly. "I guess it really doesn't matter anymore."

Travis studied her, replaying her words in his mind. But he had no idea what she'd meant by them. Her career? The foot she picked with? What could she pick with her foot for a living? Apples, beans, potatoes?

"Well, are you going to get out of my way and let me finish, or are you going to stand there and stare at me?"

Travis stepped back and she attacked Red's flank, brushing the gelding with short, angry strokes. The horse pranced nervously, nearly stepping on her foot again.

"You brush him any harder, you're going to wear right through his hide," Travis said.

Josie turned on him, wagging the brush under his nose. "I happen to have a way with horses, if you haven't noticed. I don't need your advice."

"If I hadn't have come along, you'd still be beatin' old Red on the rump, trying to rescue your foot."

"He was standing on my boot, not my foot." She returned to her task with renewed fervor.

"Use longer strokes," Travis said, stepping up behind her. He covered her hand with his and pulled the brush along the horse's flank in a smooth motion.

She froze, her hand stopping at the end of the stroke, her gaze fixed on his fingers. He felt her tremble slightly as if a current had passed between them, electric and startling in its intensity. She leaned back slightly, her body drifting against his like a soft spring breeze, one instant there and the next, gone. Travis bent his head over her shoulder and brushed his cheek against her hair.

"I—I think I can finish on my own," she said softly.

"I'll help," he replied. "Then we can go in and have some dinner."

They worked together, Travis currying Red's mane and tail while Josie brushed his coat to a soft gleam. The horse luxuriated in the attention, shaking his head proudly and pricking up his ears. When they had finished, Josie stepped back and surveyed her work.

"I *do* have a way with horses," she said.

"Yes, I believe you do." And a way with me, he added silently as they led Red back to the corral. Josie opened the gate and Travis unclipped the halter rope and slapped the chestnut on his rump. Red took off, tail high, tearing around the perimeter of the corral.

"I think he's happy. Are you happy, Red?" Josie called.

The horse must have heard her shout, because he promptly threw himself down on the ground and rolled around in the dust.

"No," Josie cried. "No, don't do that! Travis, get in there and stop him. He'll get dirty again."

"Sorry, Tink," Travis said. "Cow ponies like to roll around in the dirt. They do it all the time to keep their coat shiny."

She stared at the horse, her eyes wide with disbelief, then turned an angry gaze on him. "And you had me waste an hour giving him a bath?"

"Don't look so mad, Tink. Snake made me wash and wax six horses the first time I came to Castle Creek." He took off his hat and dropped it on her head. "Come on, tenderfoot, let's get ourselves some dinner."

Travis led her into the house and put her dinner in front of her. She ate between yawns and fell asleep during dessert, her chin cupped in her hand. Travis watched her for a long time, picking at his meal and memorizing all the tiny details of her perfect face. He would need those memories for future fantasies after she was gone.

Finally, when she nearly pitched forward into her plate of Snake's cherry pie, he pulled her up out of her chair and steered her toward the couch. She flopped down and threw her arm over her eyes. Travis pulled her boots off and dropped them on the floor, then pulled a blanket over her.

And then, as if it were the most natural thing in the world, he bent over and brushed a kiss across her soft mouth.

"Good night, sweet Josie," he murmured.

"Hmm," she moaned.

Later that night, as Travis lay awake, recalling the feel of her lips on his, she snuck into his bathroom again. He listened to the sound of her running the bath, then imagined her shrugging out of her dirty clothes and stepping into the steaming water. But this time he tried not to look as she emerged from the bathroom wrapped in a thick, terry-cloth towel.

She was right. The best thing he could possibly do was return her to Tucson and whatever life she had there. He didn't need a woman on Castle Creek. Especially not one as alluring and desirable as Josie.

# 4

"I BET YOU'LL BE HAPPY to get back to the palace, won't you, Princess?"

Josie ignored Travis's question and continued to stare out the truck window, watching the blur of scenery as it rushed by. Fast-food restaurants and self-serve gas stations, strip malls and office parks, all cluttered the landscape along the interstate, spoiling the pristine view of the mountains and the surrounding desert.

She thought she'd be happy to return to civilization, but after spending just one day at Castle Creek, the city now seemed more cluttered, more tawdry than she had remembered. As each mile passed, her apprehension grew. If only she had a palace to go home to, she wouldn't feel as frightened and alone as she did now.

The prospect of building a brand new life was now very immediate—and even more intimidating. The security of her insulated existence at Castle Creek would be gone, replaced with the everyday trials of living in the real world. If only she could ask Travis for help.

The temptation to tell him the whole truth nagged at her conscience. But something held her back, as if revealing her past would somehow taint her chances for a fresh start. Josephine Eastman, the famous figure skater, no longer existed. Everything she built from this day forward would be on a new foundation created entirely by her own hands.

"Are we almost there?" she asked quietly, turning her gaze away from the window.

He drove with one hand on the wheel, his other arm stretched casually across the back of the seat. "Almost," Travis said. "We're just a few miles outside of Tucson. You've been pretty quiet since we passed through Deadwater Gulch. Are you all right?"

Josie ran her fingers through her tangled hair and straightened her flannel shirt. As she leaned back again, she could feel the heat from his arm on the nape of her neck. She wanted to grab his hand and wrap his arm around her, like a child's security blanket to ward off the gremlins that nibbled at her confidence. "I guess I'm just a little tired," she murmured.

"Up late last night?" Travis asked.

"No. Why would you think that?"

He quirked his brow up and grinned, as if he suspected she was lying. All right, so maybe she had been up late, waiting for him to fall asleep so she could wash the smell and the dirt off her body. And after a long bath, she had spent a lingering minute or two—or maybe fifteen—staring at his bare chest above the rumpled sheets. And with that image teasing at her mind, she had slept fitfully.

But she wasn't about to tell him something he couldn't possibly know. Travis McKinnon was entirely too sure of himself, and too smug, to boot. "I think it was all that chicken herding and horse washing I did yesterday."

Travis chuckled, the warm sound flooding her senses, so much that she couldn't help but smile back at him. He playfully mussed her hair with his hand. "You're a good sport, Tink, and you did a good job."

"Do you really think so?" Josie asked, silently reveling in his compliment and his fleeting touch.

"I think so."

"I'll bet Red has never been so clean, even if it was only for a few minutes. And, you know, it was kind of fun. Different . . . but satisfying." Josie couldn't remember the last time someone had praised her work without qualifying the statement with a list of everything she'd done wrong. In fact, she knew her mother had never given her an encouraging word. But Travis had said she'd done a good job—period—and that pleased her. "I can see why you like living at Castle Creek," she said.

"Ranch work gets in your blood," he said. "The land, the animals, the freedom and solitude of working outdoors. Life is hard, but there's more satisfaction in the little everyday accomplishments."

"Do you ever miss the city?"

"Tucson?" he asked.

"No, Chicago."

He turned his curious gaze on her and she lost herself for a moment in the brilliant blue of his eyes, blue like the sky above Castle Creek. "How did you know about Chicago?" Travis asked.

"Newt and Harley mentioned it at breakfast yesterday. They said you worked for your father in some kind of business. What made you decide to give that up?"

He pulled his arm off the back of the seat and turned away as he swung the pickup off the interstate and headed into the city. She felt strangely bereft without his arm around her, without his eyes gazing into hers.

"It wasn't hard," he said, "believe me. I always knew I'd come back to Castle Creek. From the time I was just a kid, I knew that's where I wanted to live. It was kind of a fantasy of mine."

"A fantasy?" she asked.

"Mmm. Unfortunately my father doesn't share my enthusiasm for cowboy fantasies. He thinks I should be back in Chicago tending to his corporate affairs."

"But it's your life," Josie said, reaching out to place her hand on his arm. "You should be able to do what you want."

"That's a lot easier said than done, don't you think?"

He looked down at her fingers and she slowly pulled away, trying to act as if the contact was simply casual, like his arm on the back of the seat. But it was more than that. She needed to touch him, to feel his strength and confidence beneath her fingers.

"You see, my father grew up on Castle Creek," he continued. "When he was sixteen, he decided he'd had enough of ranch work and took off. He built his business from the ground up and he can't understand why I'd chose the ranch he hated over the business he loves."

"Then why did he let you spend summers here?"

"He wanted to instill in me an appreciation for the good things in life. He thought that seeing how rough life was on the ranch would make me more . . . money-hungry...more mercenary. Only problem was, his plan backfired."

"I don't think it's fair for a person to spend their life living up to someone else's expectations. Believe me, one day you'll wake up and realize you don't have a life of your own."

Travis studied her for a long moment, then turned his attention back to the street. "So what are you going to do now? They must be worried about you at the palace."

"I have a plan," Josie said. "You don't have to concern yourself about me." She turned and stared out the window. The lies were suddenly so hard to tell, yet the truth was even harder. She had no plan. Just a trip back to the hotel to collect her things, if they were still there. After that, she'd find a place to stay, a nice quiet spot where she could figure out what to do next.

Maybe she'd get a job, though for the life of her, she didn't know what qualifications she possessed. A solid double axel and a good repertoire of spins wouldn't get her much on the open employment market. She'd have to find a place to live, too. If only she could stay at Castle Creek just a little longer, until she was more certain of herself, of the life she wanted. But she couldn't do that. Her new life started here and now.

A few minutes later Travis pulled the truck into the parking lot of Ed's Equipment and Supply in a busy commercial section of Tucson. Josie looked over at him questioningly.

"I've got to drop off the transmission for the windmill," he explained. "It'll take Ed a few hours to machine the fitting, so I can take you wherever you want." He turned off the truck and pushed open his door.

Josie quickly scrambled out her side. "It's all right," she said. "I'll get out here."

Frowning, Travis circled the truck and grabbed her elbow. "No, really. I have to come back a little later and pick up the transmission, so maybe I can buy you some breakfast? Before I drop you off at the palace gates, that is."

Josie shook her head and tugged her arm from his hand. "I think it's better if we just say goodbye right now." She paused and studied the toe of her boot—actually *his* boot. Come to think of it, she was still wearing his shirt and jeans. Her gown and tiara were back at the ranch. But that was for the best, leaving the symbols of her old life behind, along with Travis McKinnon. "I—I'll send you your clothes as soon as I buy something new," she said distractedly.

Travis reached for his wallet, pulled out four twenty-dollar bills and pressed them into her hand. "Here, take this."

"I don't want your money," Josie said. "I—I'm a princess. I have plenty of money."

"Sure you are. But this is a loan, just until you can get on your feet. You can return it with the clothes."

"Thanks," Josie murmured, stuffing the money into her shirt pocket.

They stood silently in the parking lot for a long time, neither one speaking, neither one making the first effort to say goodbye. Travis reached out and took her hand again. She looked down at his long, sun-browned fingers woven through hers, so strong yet so gentle.

"There's a discount store down the street," he said. "Do me a favor and buy yourself a pair of jeans that fit before you go home. Every princess should have a good pair of blue jeans in her wardrobe."

He squeezed her hand and she tipped her chin up and met his gaze.

"Are you sure you're going to be all right?" His blue eyes filled with concern and her heart warmed. Maybe Travis McKinnon wasn't such a bad guy after all.

Josie nodded. "Thanks for everything," she said.

"No problem."

She forced a smile. "I—I better go. The palace guard has probably waited up all night long," she joked.

Travis bent toward her and brushed a kiss across her cheek. She closed her eyes and breathed in the scent of him, her hand drifting up to his shoulder. If only she could bottle that scent and take it with her. Something about it made her feel secure, protected, more sure of herself than she'd felt in a very long time.

"Take care, Princess," he murmured.

Josie stepped back and gave him a little wave, then turned and started down the sidewalk. She looked back once, just a quick glance, to find him standing in the same spot, watching her, his arm braced against the pickup. She wasn't sure how long he watched her, but by the time she was a block away, the pickup and Travis McKinnon were out of sight and gone for good.

A strange, sad feeling washed over her and she was tempted to run back to him. She'd never see Travis McKinnon again, or Newt or Harley or Snake, or any of the crazy cowboys at Javelina's. But why did she care? Before this, people had passed in and out of her life and she'd never been bothered by the loss. She'd never really needed friends. But now that she was out in the real world, alone, she wouldn't mind having a few people she could count on.

Josie forced herself to keep walking. She found the discount store right where Travis said it would be. As she walked to the front entrance, a newspaper box next to the door caught her eye. She froze, her heart stopping in her chest. When her pulse started again, she bent over and read the headline of the latest issue of the *Tucson Star* through the glass window of the box.

Olympic Figure Skater Missing. Reward Offered.

Her photo stared back at her from a rack of newspapers, the publicity photo the company used in the ice show's souvenir program, complete with rhinestone tiara. As she pressed her forehead against the window, trying to read the accompanying article, two older ladies stopped on their way to the parking lot to watch her curiously.

She straightened, then glanced down at her baggy clothes. Of course she'd elicit some strange stares. She looked like she was AWOL from a Salvation Army secondhand store. The last thing she needed now was to attract unneeded attention—especially with her face plastered on the front page of the local newspaper. A quick trip inside to purchase an inconspicuous wardrobe would be a risk, but absolutely necessary.

She sidestepped the older ladies at the door, then grabbed a shopping cart. As she wove her way through the aisles, she picked up a few curious looks but managed to duck behind the nearest rack of merchandise to evade inquiry.

Josie found the women's department, but nothing appealed to her until she spied a rack of blue jeans. Maybe Travis was right. Every princess should own a pair of jeans. She tossed a pair of Wrangler jeans—in *her* size—into the cart, then snatched up a couple of flannel shirts. After wearing one for the last day, she'd gotten used to the soft comfort and the practical warmth. Besides, they reminded her of Travis. A couple of five-dollar T-shirts, a denim jacket, and a pair of tennies completed her five-minute shopping spree and all but expended her meager budget.

She headed toward the checkout registers at a brisk pace. Her mother would have a fit if she knew Josie had set foot in a discount store. Evelyn Eastman had trained her daughter to shop only in stores that had elevator operators and uniformed doormen and no credit limits. In her dictionary, discount was a dirty word. Josie smiled to herself. From now on, she'd be spending a lot of her time in discount stores.

Though she'd had high hopes for a comfortable fantasy life, she'd come to the realization that life might not be as luxurious as she'd anticipated. After all, she had no money of her own, no job, not even a place to live. And she wasn't about to go to her mother for help. What was left on her credit cards might get her a few weeks at a decent motel, but that was about it. Strange how fantasy had a way of crumbling in the face of reality.

As she stood in line, she heard whispers behind her. She glanced nervously over her shoulder and the whispers stopped. It was only when she reached the cashier that she realized why the checkout line was dangerous territory. A rack of newspapers sat at the end of the conveyor belt—the *Tucson Star* with its inch-high headline.

She grabbed a copy of the paper and added it to a her purchases. To her relief, the cashier didn't give her second look as she counted out her change, but the two women behind her resumed their whispered exchange. Without waiting for her receipt, Josie raced out of the store, the bag of clothes tucked under her arm. She read the newspaper account of her disappearance while she hurried down the street.

Evelyn Eastman had flown into Tucson the previous night and had appeared on the late news to plead for her daughter's safe return. No ransom demands had been received yet and no trace of bronze medalist Josephine Eastman had been found, beyond her skates discovered in a trash can near the arena. She'd been missing for thirty-six hours and foul play had not been ruled out.

Foul play? No ransom demand? They thought she'd been kidnapped! Josie stopped and finished reading the article. Surely Misha had told them she had left of her own free will. She had told him she was going to find a new life; she'd made her intentions very clear. Josie groaned. But then, she'd run away before and had always come back a few hours later.

Josie opened the paper and searched for the rest of the article as she continued her walk. Evelyn was here, in Tucson, ensconced in a deluxe room at a luxury resort while she awaited word of her daughter. Once her mother found her, Josie knew for certain she'd have no chance at a life of her own. Evelyn would pacify Garner, offer him whatever he wanted to take Josie back and, by the end of the day, she'd be on the ice. She might as well hop a cab to her mother's hotel right now and save the poor Tucson police any more of Evelyn's domineering temperament.

In Evelyn's mind, Josephine was still America's princess, the sixteen-year-old girl who had stolen the the public's heart in Lake Placid. Her mother refused to acknowledge that her daughter's throne had been usurped by younger, more talented skaters, pretty young things who had captured gold and silver medals in Sarajevo and Albertville and Lillehammer. No one cared about her measly bronze medal anymore.

Except for Evelyn Eastman. Evelyn lived her life through her daughter. And once Josie gave up her identity as a skater, Evelyn would be forced to give up her own identity as a skater's mother. In a way, Josie felt a little sorry for her. After Josie's father had walked out on them when Josie was three, Evelyn had thrown all her energies and her considerable family fortune into her daughter's skating career.

Josie had been living her mother's dream for years and it was time to stop. She'd meant what she'd said to

Travis. A person had a right to live her own life. At least Travis knew what he wanted from his, he had a place to go, a real future. But Josie had nothing—except a way with chickens and horses.

She took a long, deep breath, trying to fight the sick feeling in her stomach. It didn't take much imagination to know what Evelyn would have to say about her silly fantasy. First, she'd be angry and she'd list all of Josie's shortcomings, then she'd heap on the guilt, and after that she'd weep and magnanimously admit that she was a bad mother.

And then, after standing on the receiving end of an emotional sucker punch, Josie would agree to do whatever her mother said. Not because she wanted to, but because her mother always managed to wear her down. Before long she'd have Josie convinced there was only one place in this world for her and that was on the ice.

Josie cursed. No! This time it would be different. She was stronger now and her mother *wasn't* right. There was more to life than skating and she deserved to find it—starting today. Josie glanced up and surveyed her surroundings. To her surprise, she found herself back in front of Ed's Equipment and Supply. And Travis's red pickup was still parked in front.

She wasn't sure what possessed her at that moment—whether it was a paralyzing fear of Evelyn Eastman, or a pervading realization that she still wasn't ready to face this new life of hers. But an instant later, she made her first decision. She dug a quarter out of her pocket and placed a call to the police station from a nearby pay phone. The message she left with the desk sergeant was simple. She hadn't been kidnapped, so call off the search. She gave the sergeant her social security number and her mother's birthdate as proof of who she was before she hung up the phone.

A few minutes after that Josie made the second decision of her new life. She tossed her things in the back of Travis's pickup and climbed in after them. Wedging herself into a corner, she pulled a piece of canvas over top of her and settled in for a long, bumpy ride.

Castle Creek would be as good a place as any to get her life in order. No one, including her mother, would ever think to look for her there. And she had no reason to fear that the ranch hands would blow her cover. They rarely had the time to visit Tucson and she suspected that most of them hadn't picked up a newspaper in ages. After all, she hadn't seen many newspaper delivery boys riding their bikes along the dusty back roads of Arizona at the break of dawn.

Yes, Castle Creek would be the perfect place to stay while she worked on her plan. The food was good, there was indoor plumbing, and she had plenty of time to herself.

And somehow she knew that Travis McKinnon wouldn't throw her out. After all, he'd kissed her. And that had to count for something, didn't it?

BY THE TIME Travis drove back through Deadwater Gulch, Javelina's was just opening up for lunch. Like its dinner menu, Javelina's lunch menu consisted of beef jerky, pickled eggs and chili. Right now Travis needed something—anything—to take his mind off Princess Josephine. And a bowl of Jake's five-alarm chili would provide a digestive diversion for at least the next twenty-four hours.

During the ride back from Tucson, it took all he had to keep his mind off Josie and on the road. How had this crazy, self-poclaimed princess managed to worm her way into his life in just over a day? Sure, she was pretty... all right, she was beautiful. But there was no room for a woman in his life, especially one crazy enough to believe she was a real princess.

That was it. She had to be an escapee from the local loony bin. The costume, the tiara, the convoluted story of her Russian ancestry. She truly believed she was a princess. It was definitely for the best that he'd delivered her back to where she'd come from. For all he knew, she could have murdered him in his bed and burned down the ranch house, or worse.

She was gone. So why did he feel so edgy, so restless? Women had no place in his life right now, he repeated like a mantra. But there was something about Josie that seemed to stir embers he'd long ago let die. She was tough as nails yet almost naive, aggravating and at the same time incredibly alluring. She took such pleasure in a simple compliment, yet seemed, on the surface, stubbornly self-possessed.

Princess Josephine was a complete mystery, a puzzle that he had no desire to piece together. But he suddenly regretted the fact that he would never be given the chance. He'd never know who she really was.

Travis pulled up in front of Javelina's and shut off the truck. He sat and stared out the window, watching the wind whip the main street into a roiling cloud of dust, recalling the night before last when he'd first set eyes on the princess. Of all the taverns in all the deserts, why did she have to walk into Javelina's?

Travis swore softly, then grabbed his hat from the seat and jumped out of the truck. Jeez, he was even paraphrasing Bogart over the woman!

Javelina's was empty when he walked in. In the light of day the bar looked even rougher than it did at night. Sunlight filtered through the dusty windows, piercing the ever-present cloud of cigarette smoke that hung in the air. The scarred tables and chairs were scattered haphazardly around the room as if the cowboys had just left a moment before. Travis slid onto a worn vinyl-covered stool at the bar and hitched the heels of his boots on the brass footrail.

"Where's your princess?" Jake asked, drawing a beer from the tap and sliding it in front of Travis.

Travis looked up at Jake and smiled sardonically. The rangy bartender had been one of the best horse wranglers in southwestern Arizona until a bad back had put him out of commission and into the hospitality business. He'd also taken over responsibilities as the director of Deadwater Gulch's grapevine telegraph, that venerable cowboy institution that managed to spread gossip faster than a ladies' garden club.

"She's not *my* princess," Travis replied. "And I took her back where she came from."

Jake laughed. "Too bad. The boys were hopin' you'd bring her back in. It's not every day they get to socialize with royalty."

Travis took a sip of his beer and wiped the foam off his lip with the back of his hand. "She's not royalty, Jake. And don't tell me you believe that cock-and-bull story, too."

"Shoot, I'd swear she was the Queen of England if I got a chance to eyeball that pretty face of hers again."

Travis assumed he hadn't been the only one to fall victim to the princess's beauty, but Jake's interest sparked a small flame of jealousy. "Well, she's gone, so get used to it," he said.

"Say, Chase Mitchell was in here the other day askin' after you and Castle Creek."

Travis's jaw tightened. "What did the damn buzzard say?"

"I swear, that boy's got calluses from pattin' his own back. He was braggin' on how it wouldn't be long before you had to sell out to him and his daddy."

"And what did you tell him, Jake?" As soon as he asked, Travis regretted the question. The last thing he needed was to become a willing participant in the gossip trail. What the hell did he care what the Mitchell boys had to say about him, or what Jake had to say back?

"Nothin'. Don't let those Mitchells get to you, Travis. They own half of Cochise County and got their eyes on the other half. They've wanted Castle Creek for years and they haven't managed to get their hands on it yet."

"'Yet' is the operative word here," Travis said. "And they don't want Castle Creek, they want the water underneath it. I heard their well on the south range just went dry a few months back. And I've got good water just a half mile west of there."

"Chase figures if he can get his hands on Castle Creek he'll have a place of his own to run. He don't want to share the Bar M with his big brother, and them Mitchell boys are used to getting exactly what they want. They're spoilt, that's what they are."

"Well, I've still got a year's worth of expenses left in my savings account," Travis said, "so he's going to have to wait at least that long."

"You know, there's some strange stories flying around about your plans for Castle Creek. Seems Chase has been takin' some pleasure in spreadin' these windies to the neighboring ranches."

"Well, old Chase isn't going to have to worry about my plans if I don't turn a profit this year. The only plans I'll be making is travel plans back to Chicago."

The door squeaked behind Travis, and Jake glanced up. The bartender's eyes widened and his jaw dropped. "Jeez, will ya look at that."

Travis took a sip of his beer. "What?" he asked.

"I do believe that's the Queen of England come callin'."

Travis frowned, then slowly swiveled on his bar stool, his beer glass clutched in his hand. A figure stood in the doorway backlit by the noonday sun. He squinted against the light. The door slammed shut and he blinked as his eyes adjusted.

Travis bit back a groan. No, it couldn't be! He'd left her on the sidewalk in Tucson, dressed like ragamuffin cowgirl. And here she was, back in Deadwater Gulch and, he noted, decked out in a pair of jeans that fit just right. She strolled up to the bar and sat down next to Travis. He shook his head, as if that might unseat the image from his mind. But like the night he met her, this would prove to be no mirage. This was a flesh and blood woman sitting beside him. A woman he'd managed to rid himself of not more than three hours ago.

"Aren't you going to say hello?" she asked.

Travis glared at her. "What the hell are you doing here? How did you get back to Deadwater Gulch?"

She shrugged. "Same way I got here the first time. Except this time I rode in the back of your pickup instead of your horse trailer. And I also didn't have that surly goat as company."

He slammed his glass down on the bar. "Why?" he demanded. "Why would you come back here after I drove you all the way back to Tucson?"

She folded her hands in front of her and sighed. "I changed my mind. I didn't want to go to Tucson after all."

"You changed your mind?" Travis ground his teeth. "Well, if you expect me to drive you somewhere else, Princess, you're crazier than I thought you were." He grabbed his change from the bar and pushed off the stool.

She slid to her feet. "Crazy? I'm certainly not crazy. I know exactly what I'm doing."

"Well, how do you expect to get out of Deadwater Gulch? Lacking any public transportation, the only way out of here is on foot."

She turned her startling green gaze on him, sending a current of desire shooting through his body. "I don't plan to leave," she said matter-of-factly. "I was hoping I'd be able to stay with you for a bit longer."

Travis shook his head and held up his hand to ward her off. "No way. Not again. I just got rid of you."

"You're talking like I'm some kind of communicable disease."

Travis started toward the door. "You're not my responsibility."

Josie scurried after him. "I won't be a bother, I promise. I can work for you around the ranch."

"You can work for me? And just what will you do?"

"There are a lot of things I can do. I'll take care of the chickens and I'll give Red a bath. And I—I can help out in the kitchen and I can . . . I can—"

"Princess, I need someone who can ride, someone who can tend to a windmill and fix fences. I need someone who can brand calves and shoe a horse. And Snake would have my hide if I let you anywhere near his kitchen."

"I could learn those things. If you taught me."

Travis cursed inwardly. If he let Josie back inside his house, he knew exactly what he'd want her to do—warm his bed and satisfy his carnal desires the next time she paid a midnight visit to his bathroom. But he would not allow it. Castle Creek was no place for a woman. Oh, she'd find it fascinating, maybe even charming in an idealistic way, but sooner or later the endless isolation would overwhelm her, the same way it had his fiancée. And then she'd walk out, leaving his heart as dry and barren as the low desert.

"No," Travis said.

"Why not?"

"I don't need a reason. I'm the boss and I say no."

"But you kissed me!" she cried.

Travis gasped. "What is that supposed to mean?"

"I don't know. You tell me. You're the one who was doing the kissing. I was just the kissee."

"Well, it meant nothing. Hell, I kiss my horse all the time."

"Well, then I was a definite improvement, wasn't I? Besides, I'd just be another employee, like Newt and Harley and Snake. Only you won't have to pay me. I'll work for room and board. I'll even sleep in the bunkhouse."

"You want me to give you a job?"

She nodded.

Travis grabbed her arm and steered her out of Javelina's. They stopped on the road beside his truck, his body blocking the passenger door. The wind whipped up the dust around them and Travis pulled his hat lower over his eyes. He shook his head, then cursed softly. He shouldn't, he couldn't. But staring down at her lovely face, he knew he would anyway. "All right. But before I hire you, I want you to tell me one thing."

"Anything," she said, a smile breaking across her sweet face.

"I want you to tell me that you're not really a princess."

Josie sighed impatiently. "All right, I'm really not a princess."

His gaze caught hers and held it. "What are you running away from Josie?"

She glanced away uneasily. "I thought you said one thing. That's two."

"An employer has a right to ask."

"I've never been arrested," she said. "I'm not in trouble with the law. And I'm not running away from a husband."

"Why should I believe you?" he asked.

She reached around him and yanked open the door of the truck. "I don't know. The way I see it you'll believe whatever you want to believe, no matter what I tell you." She crawled inside. "Can we go now? I'm really hungry."

With a harsh sigh, Travis slammed her door shut and rounded the truck, this time thoroughly cursing himself for his inability to control the situation. He should be dreading the prospect of having her back on Castle Creek. Yet, no matter how hard he tried to work up a little righteous anger, he couldn't help but take some pleasure in the fact that he'd have her around for a little longer.

And with Josie around, who could predict what might happen?

"ALL RIGHT, what can you do?"

Josie sat at the kitchen table, her hands folded primly

in front of her. Travis sat across from her, a pad of paper in front of him. He waited for her reply, his pencil poised, his expression expectant.

They'd finished dinner more than two hours ago and the boys had finally left for the bunkhouse. Travis had stayed in the kitchen to discuss her job responsibilities for the next day. Though she tried to concentrate on his question, her mind continually drifted in other directions—to his sun-streaked hair curled against the collar of his plaid flannel shirt and his clean smell of soap and fresh air that seemed more seductive than the most expensive cologne.

She watched his fingers as he tapped the pencil on the table and wondered if the cut she'd seen on his palm had healed. The temptation to reach out and slowly open his hand was nearly overwhelming and she imagined the feel of her lips on his skin, kissing away the hurt.

She wanted to touch him so bad she grew addled with the need. Maybe if she just reached out and casually brushed her hand against his, he might not notice. But Josie had little experience with the subtleties of this kind of infatuation. It was as if they were playing a game, advancing and retreating, dancing around each other, neither willing to admit the attraction they felt—an attraction that was ill-advised at best. After all, he wasn't just a sexy cowboy anymore, he was her boss.

"Well?" Travis prompted.

Josie forced a smile and toyed with her coffee mug, focusing her thoughts on his question. She'd never done housework before in her life, nor had she considered it necessary to learn. But suddenly she wanted more than anything to make herself useful around the ranch, to please him. "What do you need me to do?"

"Have you ever done laundry before?"

Josie sighed in relief. She hadn't personally done laundry, at least not on her own. She paid one of the corps skaters to do her laundry for her on long layovers between shows. But recently she had accompanied Misha to the coin laundry and watched him perform the task. She knew exactly how to put the quarters in the machine. "Yes," she said. "I can do laundry."

"Good. What about ironing?"

"That, too," Josie said, nodding confidently. She'd observed her mother's housekeeper iron on a number of occasions and it looked simple enough. And the wardrobe supervisor had re-ironed her costumes a number of times upon Josie's demand.

"Vacuuming?"

She shook her head, her newfound optimism waning.

Travis frowned. "You've never operated a vacuum cleaner?" He chewed on his pencil eraser, then shrugged once. "How hard can it be for you to learn?" He scribbled that task on the ever-growing list.

A nervous knot twisted in her stomach, exactly like the knot she felt before stepping on the ice in a big competition. She'd never realized the pressure the average homemaker was under.

"Dusting is easy," Travis said, "so we'll add that, too."

Josie blinked. "Dusting? Wouldn't that be a little like shoveling snow in the middle of a blizzard?"

"It just takes persistence," Travis said. "Now, you already know about the chickens. You clean the pen in the afternoons and you feed and collect eggs in the morning. What else can you do?"

"Isn't that enough?" she asked, worry creeping into her voice. She had no idea how long these tasks would take, but she wanted to make sure she did them all well and completed them on time.

"For now. We'll see how you do on these things and we'll add a few more jobs tomorrow. You don't have to worry about my room, I'll clean that myself. I'll have to teach you how to milk Winnie and feed the horses, but we'll cross that bridge later." Travis pushed away from the table and stood. "Just be sure you're out of the kitchen by three. That's when Snake starts dinner preparations and he doesn't like anyone hanging around while he's cooking. Any questions?"

"No, I think I can handle it," she replied, shooting to her feet and clutching her white-knuckled hands behind her back.

Travis strolled over to the stove and poured himself another cup of coffee. Her gaze drifted to the muscles across his back, shifting and rippling beneath the soft, plaid flannel of his shirt. "I'll be working along the north property line tomorrow fixing fences. If you have any questions, you can track down Snake and ask him."

Josie sighed dispiritedly. "I'd probably get more help if I asked Red or Winnie. Snake doesn't like to talk to me."

Travis turned, his brow arched questioningly. "Well, I'll talk to Snake and tell him to be nice to you."

She gave him a sideways glance. "Thanks," she murmured.

"For what?" he asked. "You've got a hard day's work ahead of you tomorrow."

"For believing in me," she replied. "For giving me a chance."

Travis chuckled and shook his head. "We'll see if you feel like thanking me at the end of the day." He watched her with a discerning expression. "Why did you really come back here, Josie?"

His eyes were so mesmerizing she caught herself staring, unblinking, into the pale blue depths. A current of desire suddenly sprang up between them, like a hum of static electricity in the air before a thunderstorm. "I—I knew you'd help me," she said. "And I didn't have anyplace else to go."

He reached out and placed his palm on her cheek, gently stroking the corner of her mouth with his thumb. She was afraid to move, afraid she might break the tenuous connection they'd made. Who cared that he was her boss? She wanted him to kiss her then and there, but she didn't know how to make it happen.

"One of these days you're going to tell me the truth, Josie."

She nodded, her gaze still fixed on his face. Then he pulled his hand away. "Bed and board. After a while, if you're doing a good job, the extra wage will be forty dollars a week. But remember, I'm the boss and you follow my orders."

"You're going to pay me?" Josie asked in disbelief.

"Only if you're worth it," Travis said. "Now, if I were you, I'd get some sleep. You've got a busy day coming up." Travis picked up his coffee cup and headed toward the living room.

"Travis?"

He stopped and turned around.

"You said bed and board. Does that mean I get a real bed?"

A smile curled his lips. "That's up to you. There's an extra bed in the bunkhouse that's got your name on it.

I'm sure the boys would be happy to have you. Or you can continue to sleep on the couch."

More sleepless nights on that lumpy couch? It would serve him right if she walked out the door and spent the night in the bunkhouse. "I think I'll just mosey on out there and check out the accommodations," she said.

She left Travis standing in the kitchen, his arrogant expression replaced by a frown. He might be the boss, but if he really thought he was in charge, he had another guess coming.

# 5

DUST DEVILS DANCED across the yard, kicked up by the stiff breeze that blew from midmorning to sunset, seven days a week. Already the rhythms of life on Castle Creek had been revealed to Josie. It didn't take a genius to figure out why the ranch house was always filled with dust.

The dust blew in the doors and windows, seeped into every nook and cranny and floated down onto every surface until, given time, the inside began to resemble the wide, colorless landscape outside. Josie was certain she'd been brought to Castle Creek for one reason only—to prevent the tiny stucco house from being swallowed up by the surrounding desert.

Her first morning as an employee of Castle Creek had dawned bright and clear, the sky a startling, cloudless blue, and the distant mountains a brilliant purple among a palette of neutral colors. After a hearty breakfast with the boys, she watched Travis ride out of the yard on Red, a cloud of dust trailing after him.

Josie closed the front door and wandered back to the kitchen. Snake had already deserted his domain so she sat down and reviewed her list of tasks over another cup of coffee. She reordered the list several times, adding notes of her own and sipping coffee. But overdosing on caffeine wouldn't change the inevitable. Sooner or later, she'd have to get started. And sooner or later, she'd have to face up to the fact that she might be in over her head.

She'd never felt so apprehensive in her life. At least in competition she had possessed the skills necessary to succeed. But she'd never done a lick of housework in her life, nor had she considered the fact that housework required any special knowledge. As she sat in the kitchen nursing her third cup of coffee, the vacuum cleaner sat in the corner, a menacing presence. She couldn't even bring herself to look at the washing machine and dryer. Delicate, perma-press, air fluff, pre-wash. It might as well have been written in Greek for all she understood. And she couldn't find any place for the quarters.

Why hadn't her mother taught her these things? Isn't that what a mother was for? Instead, Josie had learned how to tell sterling from silverplate, cashmere from synthetic, and old money from new. In addition, she'd learned how to be self-absorbed, stubborn and entirely unprepared for life outside the ice rink. What she wouldn't give for a few hours with Hester, the Eastman family housekeeper, right now.

Maybe it would be best to start outside the house, with the chickens and that dreaded goat. At least they didn't have dials and buttons she'd have to decipher. Travis had asked Snake to teach her how to milk Winnie and collect the eggs. She grabbed the ceramic milk pitcher from the center of the table and headed outside. But the grizzled ranch hand was nowhere to be found.

Though her search for Snake proved fruitless, she found Winnie in the shed, standing in the middle of a large stall, munching on a mouthful of hay. As Josie approached, the goat stopped chewing and regarded her with thinly disguised mistrust.

"Don't look at me like that," she warned. "I'm bigger than you."

The goat blinked indolently then went back to her meal. She was a rather large animal, about the size of a big dog, white with liver-colored spots. She had little nubs where her horns should be and droopy ears. But if a dog was man's best friend, Josie suspected this goat was determined to be her worst enemy.

"Good. I'm glad we understand each other," Josie said. "Now, I think it would be best if we developed a good working relationship. I know it's probably quite embarrassing for you to have this done, having a complete stranger grope your...well, you know. So I'm just going to place this pitcher underneath your...whatever, and you can just go right ahead and take care of this little matter."

Josie sidled over to the goat and placed the pitcher beneath her. Winnie stepped aside. Determined, Josie set it beneath her again, and this time the goat kicked the pitcher with her rear leg, sending it flying across the stall into a mound of hay.

Josie chased the pitcher down, then turned back to the goat. "All right, I'm sure it's obvious I don't know what I'm doing. But that's no reason to make me look foolish. We're both women here, and I was hoping that you'd have some respect for sisterhood."

This time when she approached with the pitcher, Winnie grabbed hold of Josie's jeans with her teeth and tried to take a bite out of the fabric, narrowly missing the leg inside.

"Just my luck," Josie muttered, scurrying out of the goat's reach. "An anti-feminist goat with a taste for denim." She sat down on a bale of hay and cupped her chin in her hand.

"This is hard enough for me without you making it harder. I'm just trying to find a place here. And if you knew how desperate I was to do a good job, you wouldn't be giving me so much trouble. So, I guess you're going to force me to do this the regular way."

The goat's head snapped up and she bleated as if she understood what Josie had said.

"I'm not completely ignorant about these things," Josie said, waving the pitcher in Winnie's direction. "I have a basic idea of how cows are milked and I'd assume that goats operate the same way. If you'd prefer to do this the traditional way, then we will. But it's going to be as embarrassing for you as it is for me. And it will probably be painful, as well."

Josie stood and approached Winnie again, trying to appear confident yet casual, as if she'd milked goats as many times as she'd laced her skates. Winnie lowered her head, narrowed her big brown goat eyes and bared her teeth. She'd heard once that wild animals could sense a human's fear—and though Winnie was of the domestic variety, Josie was certain there was a cougar somewhere in the goat's genealogy.

As Josie attempted to corner the goat, Winnie simply circled the stall, the bell around her neck clanking a taunt. She was surprisingly nimble, staying just out of Josie's reach in a bizarre game of tag. After five trips around the perimeter of the stall, Josie decided to give up. She'd been outwitted by a barnyard animal.

Josie paced the width of the stall, the goat following her movements with wary eyes. "I don't think you truly understand my position here," Josie stated, trying to remain calm. "Either you let me milk you, or essentially, my life is over. I'll be forced to go back to Tucson. I'll have no job, no money. I'll have to join another ice show. Only this time I'll have to wear one of those awful costumes with the huge animal heads. You have no idea what that will do to me. I'd rather be run over by a Zamboni than wear one of those big heads."

At least this made some impression on Winnie. Josie wasn't sure, but it looked like Winnie was smiling at her. Well, maybe she was getting somewhere now.

"Talkin' to that goat ain't gonna git her milked."

Josie spun around. Snake stood in the stall opening, watching her with an unnerving eye. She wasn't as surprised to see him as she was to hear him string more than two words together. "I was just getting Winnie ready for . . . the milking. But she preferred to wait for you."

Snake stepped inside, a bucket in his hand. He grabbed a three-legged stool from the corner of the stall. "She tell you that?" he challenged.

Josie laughed nervously. "No. Of course not."

"I thought maybe in your conversation, she mighta told you that."

"Well, she didn't," Josie snapped. "She also didn't tell me how to milk her. You're supposed to do that."

"Are you sure you wanna learn? Winnie can be mighty unpleasant when she wants to be."

"I am not going to let some stubborn goat get my . . . goat," Josie said. "Now, show me how to milk her."

Snake grabbed Winnie's collar and gently maneuvered her into the corner of the stall. He dropped the stool beside her and the bucket beneath her, then, leaning against her with his shoulder, reached down and began to take care of business.

"Come here and give it a go-round," Snake said.

Josie hesitantly approached the goat. Winnie bleated once and bared her teeth. Josie stood behind Snake and stuck out her tongue.

"Grab hold down there, one in each hand," he instructed. "Then squeeze down from the top, one finger at a time, tuggin' a little, too."

Josie winced and knelt down beside the goat, then did as she was told. A stream of milk hit the bucket with a sharp ping and she jumped back.

"Oh, my," she breathed.

"You got it," Snake said. "Now set down here and finish the job."

Josie switched places with Snake, took a deep breath and tried it again. In a few minutes she had a small pool of frothy goat's milk in the bottom of the pail. She glanced over her shoulder at Snake. "I—I know we didn't get off on the right foot, but I was hoping we might get past that. I really need to make this job work."

"When are you goin' to tell Travis who you really are?"

Josie froze. Winnie raised her head from the pile of hay she'd been devouring and looked at Josie with the same penetrating stare Snake had fixed on her. "What do you mean?" Josie asked softly.

"I know who you are. I saw you once. In Dallas. 'Bout seven years ago."

Josie gasped. "You're a figure skating fan?" The words were already out of her mouth by the time she realized she'd given herself away. For all she knew, he'd seen someone that looked like her in some old honky-tonk. "I—I mean—"

"And I was watchin' when you got your medal in Lake Placid. You shoulda gotten a gold, or a silver at least."

"It was the East German judge," Josie explained hesitantly. "My mother had an absolute fit. She sent a case of shaving cream to the woman's hotel room." She smiled and shook her head. "That's Evelyn. Always the last word."

"And I was watchin' when you fell twice in Sarajevo."

Josie let out a long breath. "I just couldn't seem to find the ice that night," she explained. "God, I was so scared and embarrassed. I never wanted to skate again. But, of course, my mother had the final word on that one, too. I was supposed to take the gold medal in Sarajevo and I went into the free skate in twenty-first place. It would have meant endorsements, a big ice show contract. I placed fifteenth. She still talks about it."

For a long time her mother had accused her of falling on purpose. Now, as she looked back on it, maybe her mother had been right. All she'd wanted was a chance to step away from the pressure, an excuse to be someone other than Josephine Eastman. She'd thought that winning would provide an escape. When it hadn't, she'd tried losing. And when that hadn't helped, she'd just accepted that she'd never be happy with her life and vowed to make everyone around her as miserable as she was.

Until now. For the first time in memory, she felt happy, content, comfortable with herself.

"So, when are you gonna tell him?" Snake repeated.

Josie bit her bottom lip and went back to work.

"I—I wasn't planning to. I didn't think it made a difference. And I certainly didn't expect to find a figure skating fan in the middle of the Arizona desert. That life is in my past and it doesn't have anything to do with this life."

"Jest because you ignore it, don't make it go away," Snake said. "The past has a way of sneakin' up on a feller. Or a gal."

"You can't tell him," Josie said. "I don't want to be that person anymore. I want to start fresh. Being Josephine Eastman comes with all sorts of expectations of perfection. But being just plain Josie is a whole lot easier. Besides, what difference does it make?"

"That depends on your intentions regardin' Travis, I s'pose."

"My intentions? I don't understand."

"I expect you will, sooner or later. And so will Travis."

Josie frowned, his meaning unclear. "But you won't tell him, will you? He'll take me back to Tucson right away. At least give me a chance to prove I can do this job. Then I promise I'll tell him everything."

Snake considered her request for a long moment, scratching his chin and studying her sagaciously. "I ain't the kind to feed off my range, but I promised Smilin' Jack I'd watch over the boy, and I mean to keep that promise. Do we have ourselves an understandin'?"

Josie nodded. "We do."

Snake tipped his hat. "Your word's good with me. Now, I got me some work to do and so do you."

He turned and started out, but Josie's words stopped him.

"You know, Snake, when I first met you, you scared the stuffing out of me. But you're not all that bad. In fact, you're a real gentleman." Josie graced him with her most charming smile. She thought she saw a blush creep up the old man's leathery cheeks.

"Don't you be tellin' that windy to no one else, you hear?" he threatened, shaking a crooked finger at her. "I got me an image to uphold."

Josie giggled. "I know what you mean, Snake. And I'll keep quiet. You can depend on it."

"YOU DON'T want to go in there," Snake warned.

Travis groaned and flopped down in the rocking chair next to Snake's. He covered his face with his hands, scrubbing at his dust-reddened eyes. He'd come in for lunch, hoping to have a chance to check up on Josie. "Why? What's wrong?"

"The last time I went inside, she was beatin' on the vacuum cleaner with the mop. She flooded the kitchen with suds from the washin' machine. Somehow the refrigerator got unplugged and your strawberry ice cream is leakin' out the freezer door. And you're goin' to be wearing pink underwear for a spell."

Travis slanted a glance in Snake's direction. "Is that it?"

Snake pushed out his bottom lip and thought on it for a while. "Yep. 'Cept for your fancy black John B.," he said.

"What happened?"

"She washed it. In the washin' machine. You left it settin' on top and she took that to mean it needed washin'."

Travis kicked his feet up on the railing and studied the toe of his boot. "Well," he said, "I never did like that black hat in the first place. Too citified. I'm more a brown hat type of guy."

They sat on the bunkhouse porch for a long while, neither one speaking, Snake whittling one of his horses and Travis trying to figure out how to handle his newest employee.

"I don't mean to wedger in," Snake finally said, "but why did you bring that little gal back here?"

"I don't think she has anyplace else to go," Travis said.

"That ain't the only reason, is it?"

"What is that supposed to mean?" Travis asked.

"Jest that she's as pretty as a red heifer in a flowerbed, if you haven't noticed."

Travis quirked his brow. "I've noticed. I'm not blind."

In fact, he saw all too well. There had been times when she'd turned in his direction and her beauty had taken his breath away. He'd catch himself staring, wondering if there was another woman in the world who could affect him the way she did. He could spend a week—heck, a month—looking at her and still not get enough.

"But that's not why I brought her back here," Travis continued. "She's running from something, but she won't tell me what it is. Could be trouble. She's not a princess, you know."

"Yep," Snake said. "I figgered that right off."

"Who do you suppose she is? Do you think she's running away from a husband? Or maybe a boyfriend? She could be married for all we know."

"Does it make a difference?" Snake asked, eyeing him shrewdly.

"Hell, yes. I don't want some guy showing up here, guns blazing, to retrieve his runaway wife."

"Why don't you jest ask her?"

Travis chuckled. "I have. She doesn't want to talk about it. Besides, I can't tell whether she's giving me the truth anyway."

"I don't think she's married," Snake said.

"You don't?" Travis couldn't eliminate the hopeful tone from his voice. He didn't want her to be married, though he really didn't know why it should make a difference. He had no intention of getting involved with her, married or not.

"That little gal wouldn't be much use as a wife, anyway," Snake said. "She cain't even work a vacuum cleaner."

"Josie's good at other things," Travis said.

"Why don't you tell me just what Josie is good at and let me be the judge?" Snake replied.

Travis stared across the yard, fixing his gaze on the house. She was incredibly good at being a woman. An alluring, enchanting wisp of a woman who appeared to him every night in his dreams, leaving him to wonder what passion he might find in her if given the chance. She would be good in his arms, of that he was certain.

"Don't worry," Travis murmured, reining in his imagination. "Sooner or later, I'll find something she can do." He sat up and stretched his arms over his head. "So, you think I should go in there?"

"Somebody's got to. An' it ain't gonna be me, that's fer damn sure."

Travis let out a long breath, then pushed to his feet. He took the bunkhouse steps one at a time, dreading the woman he'd find inside the ranch house more than the disaster. She'd probably find a way to blame him for making a mess of things and all he'd be thinking about would be kissing her senseless.

"The gal's got heart," Snake commented. "I wouldn't be too hard on her."

Travis shot him an incredulous look. "Since when have you been a member of her fan club?"

"Maybe you could take 'er into Bisbee fer lunch. I need a few things from the grocery and there ain't a gal I know who don't like to shop. 'Sides, that'll give me a chance to clean up the mess she made."

"Thanks for the advice," Travis replied. As he walked to the house, he pondered Snake's sudden change in attitude. If he didn't know better, he'd swear Snake was falling under her spell just like Newt and Harley had.

Travis found Josie on her hands and knees, mopping up melted ice cream from the kitchen floor. As Snake had warned him, the house was a disaster, but she looked worse. He was tempted to tiptoe back out again and let her put herself and the kitchen back in order in her own time, but it looked like she had at least a good day's work left in front of her. Rather than retreat, he cleared his throat.

She turned around so quickly, her knee skidded on the ice cream and she landed on her backside. Her gaze darted between the mess in the kitchen and his expression, which he carefully schooled into indifference.

"So," he said, trying to sound cheerful, "how's it going?"

She gaped at him, her eyes wide. "How's it going?" she repeated. "How's it going?" The second time her voice was almost a shout. "Fine. Wonderful, in fact. It's going just—"

She rested her elbows on her knees and covered her face with her hands. At first Travis thought she was laughing, but then he realized he was wrong. Oh, Lord, she was crying. And he could handle just about anything except a woman in tears.

He walked across the kitchen, squatted down beside her, and reached out to pat her on her shoulder. "Aw, Josie. Don't cry. I—I think you're doing a fine job. A really fine job."

She dropped her hands into her lap and stared at him in disbelief, a tear popping from the corner of her eye. She brushed it away angrily. "Have you lost your mind as well as your eyesight? I haven't managed to do a single thing right all morning long." She held up her hand. "Wait, that's not exactly right. I did milk Winnie, but then I tripped leaving the stall and dumped the milk all over my shoes."

Travis chuckled, then hitched his hands under her arms and lifted her to her feet. "No, I haven't lost my mind, but if you stay here much longer, I'm afraid *you* might. Come on, Tink, I'm taking you to town."

"No!" she moaned, pulling out of his grasp. "You have to give me another chance. I can't go back. Not yet."

Travis placed his hands on her shoulders and gently pushed her down on the bench next to the table, then retrieved a damp rag from the kitchen sink. "I'm not taking you to Tucson," he said as he wiped her sticky hands. "I'm taking you to Bisbee, for lunch. After that, we've got some shopping to do. You do know how to shop, don't you?"

She sniffled. He pulled his bandanna out of his pocket and wiped at her runny nose and eyes.

She managed a smile. "I'm good at shopping," she said with a hiccup.

"I'll even let you drive," Travis said.

Josie looked at him with incredulous emerald eyes, then swallowed hard. "Drive?"

Travis studied her panicked expression. "You do know how to drive, don't you?" The tears welled in her eyes again, but he stopped them from spilling over with his bandanna. "Jeez, Josie, will you cut that out? If you can't drive, I'll teach you. Just don't cry."

"I'm not crying," Josie murmured, snatching the bandanna from his hand. "I never cry."

"What do you call that leaking out of your eyes, then?"

She frowned. "I mean, I've never cried like this before."

Travis nodded. "Usually you pitch a royal fit when you're mad. Shoot, I can deal with your temper better than I can deal with your tears."

She dabbed at the corners of her eyes and forced a smile. "I'm learning how to control my temper now. But if it would make you feel better, I'd be happy to throw some china and break some glassware."

"I'd be happy if you'd just stop crying."

She drew a ragged breath. "I don't know what's gotten into me. I usually keep my feelings all bottled up inside. I'm not sure why I cried now, except that it seemed to be the right thing to do." Josie blew her nose, then handed him the bandanna. "I feel really good now. Refreshed. I should cry more often." She glanced around the kitchen then sighed. "I guess I'd better finish cleaning up."

"Leave it," Travis ordered.

"But I think I should—"

Travis placed his finger over her lips. "I'm the boss here and the boss says leave it. Now, go get your jacket and meet me at the truck for your first driving lesson.

After you learn how to operate the truck, the washing machine and the vacuum cleaner will seem like a piece of cake."

BY THE TIME they reached the tiny town of Bisbee, Josie had all but mastered the art of driving. She knew the accelerator from the brake, had turned five different corners, and could shift from Park into Drive and back again. Once they left the dirt back roads, Travis took over, driving the last leg on the highway into town. At the same time, he answered all her questions about the surrounding landscape.

Besides learning how to operate the pickup, Josie learned that the mountains she looked at every morning from the porch were called the Swisshelm Mountains. She knew that the gnarled trees in front of the house were cottonwoods. And she could now tell mesquite from cholla, creosote from prickly pear, and juniper from sagebrush.

But nothing had prepared her for Bisbee. She'd expected a town much like Deadwater Gulch, remote and weather-beaten. What she got was a picturesque Victorian town perched on the side of a hill, its steep winding streets tracing paths through a charming patchwork of architectural styles. Redbrick and stucco buildings housed a variety of shops, craft galleries and other tourist attractions.

Travis's first stop was a small store that specialized in Western wear. He helped Josie out of the truck, laced his fingers through hers, and led her to the door. A warm, safe feeling settled around her heart and she felt as if she were still in high school, holding hands with the most handsome boy in class. It was nearly impossible not to have a little crush on the cowboy that walked beside her. What harm could a slight infatuation be?

But as soon as she saw the endless racks of cowboy hats inside the store, her heart plummeted and that cozy feeling dissolved. The store was wall-to-wall hats! Every style and color a cowboy could possibly desire. How could she stand among all these hats without telling him what she'd done? Sooner or later he'd find his black hat missing and then he'd begin to ask questions. She had no doubt that the trail of evidence would lead directly back to her.

"I'm sorry," Josie murmured, standing beside him as he perused a long rack of hats.

He glanced over at her and arched his brow. "For what?"

She twisted her fingers in front of her. "I didn't mean to do it," she cried. "I mean, I meant to do it, but I didn't realize what I was doing."

A grin curled the corner of his mouth. "What did you do, Josie?"

"I—I washed your black hat," she said, her words coming out in a rush. "I'm sorry, but I—"

"I know. Snake told me."

"You know?"

He shrugged. "Nothing much goes on at Castle Creek that I don't find out about."

"So you came here to buy a new hat?" She held up the price tag and peered at it. Her eyes widened. "Oh, dear. One hundred dollars for a hat? How could I have done something so stupid? I—"

"Josie, we're not here to buy me a new hat," Travis explained. "Besides, I bought that hat in Chicago before I came to Castle Creek and I've decided I'm really not a black hat kind of guy. We're here to buy *you* a hat."

"Me?" Josie asked. "I don't need a hat."

"If you're going to work on Castle Creek, you'd better look like you belong there." He placed a buff-colored hat on top of her head. "This is a nice one." He turned her toward the mirror. "What do you think? That tiara of yours isn't really made to protect your head from the sun and the rain. I think this is a much better choice, don't you?"

Josie took the hat off and stroked the soft felt, then dropped it back on the rack. "I can't," she said softly. "I don't have the money to buy this."

He put the hat back on her head and adjusted the brim. "You don't have to buy it. I'll buy it for you."

"I can't accept a gift like this!" she cried, snatching the hat from her head.

"It's not a gift. Call it part of the uniform." He snatched it from her hands and put it back on her head again, this time tugging it down firmly and holding the crown down with his hand. "When summer comes, we'll have to get you a straw hat. They're lighter and cooler."

"Summer?" she asked, gazing up into his eyes from beneath the wide brim. Did he really expect her to be at Castle Creek when the weather turned warmer? Was he asking her to stay? Somehow she'd just assumed she'd be gone by then, most likely tossed out on her ear for burning down the ranch house—or even gone of her own will. But now she had cause to wonder.

Travis glanced away uneasily. "Do you see anything else you'd like?"

"No," she replied softly. "This is too much already."

She stood silently beside him as he paid for the hat. Without even realizing it, they'd fallen into an easy friendship, a friendship that she couldn't imagine abandoning. A friendship that might last the winter and spring, and maybe even through the summer.

He'd given her a place to sleep and a job to do. When she'd cried, Travis had mopped up her tears. When she hadn't known how to drive, Travis had taught her. And now he was buying her a cowboy hat. This was not the behavior one usually expected from a boss.

"If you were a serious cowgirl, you'd take that hat to a hat creaser. He'd give your hat the right look for your head. Snake knows how to crease a hat, so he can show you." He quirked a shy smile in her direction. "Just don't put it in the washing machine."

Josie returned his grin haltingly. "I'm not putting anything else in that machine. It turns everything pink ... including your underwear."

Travis placed his hand on her back and steered her out the door. "After Snake teaches you how to crease a hat, we're going to have him give you a lesson on separating the laundry."

"Separating it from what?" Josie asked.

"Never mind," Travis said. "Let's get something to eat."

They strolled the town before having a late lunch in the lovely dining room of the old Copper Queen Hotel. Many of the turn-of-the-century buildings had been beautifully restored, including the hotel, making Josie feel as if she'd somehow stepped back in time a hundred years. Travis told her stories of the boomtown days when Bisbee had been one of the most prosperous cities in Arizona, "the" place to stop between New Orleans and San Francisco. He told her how the boomtowns had turned into ghost towns when the copper mines had played out. And to Josie's surprise, she'd managed to forget the morning's disasters, and the uneasy talk of the future, and lose herself in the sights and sounds of the old mining town.

"I want to show you something," Travis said as they sped down the highway on the way home.

"You've shown me so much already," she said. "I've had a wonderful time, seeing the town, visiting the shops, learning to drive."

Travis swung the truck off the main highway onto a narrow dirt road. "This is something different."

"What?" Josie asked.

He smiled. "I'm taking you to see a miracle," he said.

She watched him out of the corner of her eye, wondering at his odd shift in mood. But she had stopped trying to figure out Travis McKinnon a few hours after she'd met him. The man was a study in contradictions. First he was angry, then aloof, then he was understanding and indulgent, and now all of a sudden he seemed to be filled with a quiet excitement that was almost contagious.

She had once thought him dangerous, but now the description seemed strangely incongruous with the man she was coming to know. He had his dangerous moments, but beneath it all was a goodness and a strength of character that she couldn't ignore. He was a difficult man to understand and an even more difficult man to resist. Right now, the only danger Travis McKinnon posed was to her heart.

They bumped down a long dirt road for nearly fifteen minutes before he stopped the truck. "Come on," he said, taking her hand and pulling her toward his side of the cab. He spanned her waist with his hands and lifted her out of the truck, then left one hand resting possessively on her hip. They walked together toward a fence line that ran parallel to the road, five strings of barbed wire on six-foot-high metal stakes.

"What do you see?" he asked.

Josie glanced around. She really hadn't been paying attention. Her mind had been distracted by the easy way they seemed to fit together, his arm around her waist, her shoulder tucked against him.

"Well?" he prompted.

"I—I see a fence. You've got fences just like this at Castle Creek. What's so special about this one?"

Travis laughed then pushed her new hat back on her head. "Look beyond the fence, Tink."

Josie did as she was told, stepping closer to peer through an opening between the barbed wire. "I see tall, green grass." She turned back to Travis, hoping that this time she'd given him the right answer.

"What you see is more precious than gold to a rancher," Travis replied.

"Grass?" Josie asked. "I think I'd rather have the gold."

"It's not just grass, Tink, it's the soil that supports the grass and the water that supports the soil, the whole ecosystem. What you're looking at is the way this part of Arizona, and Castle Creek, used to look a hundred years ago, before the land was overworked and over-grazed."

Josie frowned. "I don't understand," she said. "This is just grass. It grows everywhere."

"Not like this, and not on Castle Creek. It used to. When the first settlers came here the land was a grassy savannah, not a dusty desert."

"What happened? Was there a drought?"

"The early ranchers put too many head of cattle on too little land. The herds ate up all the grass, and the topsoil that supported the grass blew away."

"Well, I'm pretty sure I know where it is," Josie teased. "It's all inside your house."

Travis glanced down at her. With a grin, he gently pulled her back into the circle of his arm. "When the grass goes, the grazing does, too. Slowly the pastures get clogged with brush and trees, mostly juniper and piñon, invasive vegetation that uses all the water. Without water, the grass can't come back."

"And this is the way you'd like Castle Creek to look?" Josie asked.

Travis nodded. "This is the way it *can* look."

"You want to plant some grass?"

His arm tightened around her shoulders. "More than that. First, most of the scrubby trees and brush have to be cleared. The vegetation needs to be burned every so often to give the grass a chance to establish itself. Some of the seed is still there from fifty or a hundred years ago just waiting for the right time to sprout. And where it doesn't come back on its own, I can plant new."

His enthusiasm spilled over into his deep voice and his pale eyes and the set of his smile. And suddenly she realized that she wanted this for him as much as he did. "The more grass you have, the more cows you can have," she said.

"Actually, I'd have to reduce the size of my herd for a while, to keep the new grass from being overgrazed. I'd have to rotate pastures more often. But the cattle will be healthier and the fertility rate will go way up because of it."

"So when are you going to start?" Josie asked.

Travis shrugged and sighed. "I don't know if I am. Right now, as far forward as I can look is a year."

"How long will it take to do this on Castle Creek?"

"A lifetime," Travis said. "Twenty, thirty years. Maybe more."

Josie gasped. "But that's forever!"

"Yep," he murmured. "But I'd really like to see it in my lifetime."

She looked out at the pasture, the long grass waving in the wind. It shimmered under the sun, like a vast inland sea dotted with small islands of cottonwoods. He was right. It was better than gold. She tried to imagine sitting on the porch at Castle Creek, looking out over land as alive as this was. "So would I," she said softly.

She felt his arm slip from her shoulders to her waist. Slowly, he turned her to face him, resting his hands on her hips. Josie stared at his chest for a long moment, then hesitantly glanced up to meet his gaze. He watched her, his blue eyes suddenly intense, clouded with a color she'd never seen before. Slowly, he reached up and brushed her cheek with the back of his hand.

Josie drew a deep breath and held it, afraid to move knowing that it might somehow break the connection they'd made. It seemed so natural, just the next logical step from all the times they'd touched during the day, at first so casual and now more intimate.

Closing her eyes, she tilted her chin, inviting his kiss. He pulled her hat off and she heard it drop to the ground, and then his mouth was on hers, not soft and gentle, but firm and full of unfaltering possession.

He slid his arm around her waist and tugged her body against his, molding her shape against him until every nerve inside her hummed. Her head filled with sound: her heart beating, his harsh breathing, and the wind rustling in the grass around them. She wanted to drag him down to the ground and pull him on top of her, but she seemed unable to move, unable to reason.

He wove his fingers through her hair, pressing her mouth to his as he had done with her body. His lips moved from her cheeks to her eyelids, across her forehead, and then back again, restlessly seeking, demanding something more.

And then, as suddenly as it had begun, it stopped. She opened her eyes and gazed up at him through a haze. A pained look froze on his handsome face, a look of sheer regret. She placed her hand on his chest and felt his heart thudding a rapid beat.

He drew a shaky breath and brushed her fingers away. "We'd better go."

She carefully schooled her expression, unwilling to reveal her confusion. The current that had seemed to flow between them, so electric and arousing, was gone now. He didn't want her, not as much as she wanted him.

As she pulled back, all her insecurities flooded her mind, instantly hardening her heart, protecting her from hurt. Like armor, she steeled herself against all the warmth and closeness she felt toward him.

For a short time, he'd made her feel as if she had a place at Castle Creek. Even amid all the disasters, he'd given her a chance to succeed, an opportunity to prove herself. And she'd fallen into his trap, believing that she might be able to carve out a future for herself, might someday find a home at the ranch.

Josie cursed her stupidity. She didn't need him. She didn't need anyone. She was in charge of her own life and thinking there could ever be a future at the ranch, a future with him, was pure folly. She had her own dreams, and however exciting she found his plans for Castle Creek, however comfortable she may become on the ranch, she would leave as soon as she'd decided what to do with her new life.

Castle Creek wasn't *her* dream, it was his, and she'd do well to remember that fact. After all, hadn't she learned her lesson? She wasn't about to waste another minute of *her* life living someone else's dreams.

# 6

TRAVIS SAT atop Red and looked out over the herd as the cattle swarmed down a hill toward a dry creek bed. The sounds of the dogs barking and the cowboys shouting drifted back to him on the breeze. Snake was out ahead, riding point. Harley rode swing about a third of the way back and Newt was on the opposite flank, not far from Travis. Castle Creek's three border collies, the only animals who were officially granted names on the ranch, scooted around the herd, obeying the whistles and commands of the cowboys.

Though riding drag was the dirtiest and most disagreeable job on the trail, Travis preferred it. It was good, hard work and a challenge to keep the lazy and weaker critters in line, all the while fighting a cloud of dust kicked up by hundreds of hooves.

And then there were times like these, when he could sit a spell at the top of a rise and look down on all that he owned . . . and dream about the possibilities of better times.

Moving the herd was a tiring and frustrating affair, especially with only four riders and more than four hundred head of cattle to contend with. Since his range management plan called for frequent shifts in grazing land and he couldn't afford any more full-time hands, they moved the cattle in small bunches, usually spending at least four days at the task. He'd hire seasonal help at roundup time and let them go as soon as the hard work was done. Thankfully, this was the last short-handed move before spring roundup. In just a few weeks the cows would begin to drop their calves and the real work would begin.

As soon as the last calf was born and could walk, the cowboys would gather the herd again. The bulls would be cut out and penned. Calves would be separated from their mothers, branded and inoculated, and the males castrated. Then most would be turned back out to find their mothers and await their fate. As the season progressed, the steers would be shipped, along with the old and unproductive heifers and the weaker female calves. The rest of the calves would be left with the herd to build a heartier stock.

Travis had come to Castle Creek just before spring roundup the year before and it had been a miserable time. Only about fifty percent of the heifers had healthy calves, putting the ranch in the hole from the get-go. He had vowed to make the next year more successful— or die trying.

He'd spent the year culling the herd, improving their health with better grazing, and bringing in three new bulls to strengthen the bloodlines. All he had left in his savings now was enough to pay wages for another year. If the herd didn't produce at a better rate this time around, he might as well cash in his chips and get while the gettin' was good.

Snake rode to the top of the rise and reined his horse next to Travis's. He looked down at the scene below, then casually rolled himself a cigarette. Travis was almost afraid to ask, but he did. "What do you think? How does it look?"

Snake nodded slowly, never taking his eyes off the herd. He clamped down on the cigarette with his teeth and scratched a match on his boot heel, then lit up. "It looks good. I'm not one to count my chickens, but I will say they're fat and sassy, so the younguns should be healthy. It's the best the bunch has looked in a long time."

Travis closed his eyes and relaxed in his saddle. Snake didn't have to say more. This was the first positive sign Travis had and he wanted to savor it. All his worrying about herd management and his grazing plan might just pay off. A good roundup would buy him at least another year beyond this one, barring any unforeseen natural disasters.

His mind wandered to an image of Josie and he bit back a curse. It was awful hard to contemplate disaster and not think of Josie at the same time. And it wasn't just her housekeeping skills, it was the effect she had on his senses that made her a disaster waiting to happen.

Though he had tried to banish the memory from his brain, he couldn't forget the powerful, nerve-rattling kiss they'd shared on the road back from Bisbee, a kiss he had wanted to go on forever. And given a few more seconds with his mouth on hers, he wouldn't have been able to stop himself. As it was, he'd replayed those few moments over and over again until he was certain he'd go mad with wanting her.

But he couldn't have Josie. Having her would be the biggest mistake he'd ever make. It would be so easy to fall in love with her and for all the wrong reasons. She was beautiful and sexy, and he hadn't been around a woman as desirable as her for a very long time. Lust, pure and simple. Beyond that, she was a mess, the kind of woman who needed help and protection.

But he was not some love-blind knight on a white horse, ready to charge to her rescue. And he refused to let himself feel more than just mild attraction to Josie. She was a woman, and there was no place for women, or the distractions they provided, on Castle Creek. Sure, she'd stayed for almost two weeks, but he might as well face facts. Sooner or later, she'd leave.

"I'm headin' back to the house after we get these critters settled," Snake said. "You comin' back or are you gonna ride fence with the boys?"

Bracing his hand on his saddle horn, Travis leaned forward and rubbed Red on the neck. "You aren't scared to go back there alone, are you?" he asked.

Snake shifted uneasily in his saddle, then examined his cigarette with great concentration before he answered. "I just ain't sure what I'm gonna find, that's all. She's been there alone all mornin'."

"Come on," Travis chided. "You've got to admit, she hasn't been doing that bad lately."

"Compared to what? A horse in high heels? That girl don't know sic 'em about housework."

"She's trying. And at least she's stopped throwing those little tantrums of hers."

Snake snorted. "Now she just gets all runny-eyed when she's mad. I cain't abide a woman in tears."

"So what do you want me to do?" Travis asked. "Fire her? Hell, I'm not paying her yet, how can I fire her?"

"Shoot, I'd be happy if you'd admit why you're keepin' her around," Snake commented.

"And why is that?"

Snake shrugged. "'Cause you got yerself a powerful case of calico fever, I'd say."

Travis glared at him. "For point man, you ain't doin' much pointin' sittin' up here. Why don't you get back down there and give Harley and Newt a hand?"

Snake smiled and tipped his hat, then nudged his horse with his heels. "See ya back at the house," he called as he rode down the hill.

Travis pushed his hat back, untied his bandanna from around his neck and wiped at his dirty face with the damp cloth. The only way to put her out of his mind was to stay as far away from her as possible. Hell, he'd started sleeping with his back to the bathroom door just to avoid the temptation of looking at her every night as she emerged from her shower. He'd even considered buying a lock for his bedroom door, or maybe banishing her to sleep in the bunkhouse with the boys.

But no matter how hard he tried to put her out of his mind, he still found himself inexplicably drawn back to the ranch house in the middle of the workday, and always with a valid excuse. In fact, he'd already decided that he'd have to go back early today to make out the week's payroll. Saturday night had rolled around once again and Newt and Harley would be off to Javelina's right after dinner. They needed pocket change for pool and poker.

Travis picked up the reins and clucked his tongue, directing Red down the steep hill toward the herd. Snake had already opened the barbed-wire gate to the northeast pasture and Newt and Harley were driving the cattle in that direction when Travis rode up.

As Newt closed the gate on the last straggler, Snake gave the boys a wave and set out at a trot for the ranch house. Travis, Newt and Harley watched the herd for a long while, their horses lined up along the barbed-wire fence. The boys sensed, as Snake had, that the cattle looked good and they both took a certain pride in that fact, knowing they'd shared in the accomplishment.

# N IMPORTANT MESSAGE
# ROM
# HE EDITORS OF HARLEQUIN®

ear Reader,

ecause you've chosen to read one of our
ine romance novels, we'd like to say
thank you"! And, as a **special** way to
hank you, we've selected <u>four more</u> of the
ooks you love so well, **and** a lovely
ecklace to send you absolutely *FREE!*

lease enjoy them with our compliments...

Bught Dawn-Ford

Editor,
Temptation

?.S. And <u>because</u> we value our
ustomers, we've attached something
xtra inside ...

EDITOR'S
**FREE
GIFT
SEAL**
THANK YOU

PEEL OFF SEAL AND
PLACE INSIDE

# HOW TO VALIDATE
## YOUR
# EDITOR'S FREE GIFT
# "THANK YOU"

**1.** Peel off gift seal from front cover. Place it in space provided at right. This automatically entitles you to receive four free books and a lovely gold-tone necklace.

**2.** Send back this card and you'll get brand-new Harlequin Temptation® novels. These books have a cover price of $3.25 each, but they are yours to keep absolutely free.

**3.** There's no catch. You're under no obligation to buy anything. We charge nothing—ZERO—for your first shipment. And you don't have to make any minimum number of purchases—not even one!

**4.** The fact is thousands of readers enjoy receiving books by mail from the Harlequin Reader Service®. They like the convenience of home delivery...they like getting the best new novels before they're available in stores...and they love our discount prices!

**5.** We hope that after receiving your free books you'll want to remain a subscriber. But the choice is yours—to continue or cancel, anytime at all! So why not take us up on our invitation, with no risk of any kind. You'll be glad you did!

**6.** Don't forget to detach your FREE BOOKMARK. And remember...just for validating your Editor's Free Gift Offer, we'll send you FIVE MORE gifts, *ABSOLUTELY FREE!*

---

### *FREE BEAUTIFUL 20" GOLD-TONE CHAIN!*
*You'll love this 20" gold-tone chain! The necklace is beautifully crafted in a classic herringbone design and comes in its own red velvet draw-string pouch! And it's yours free as added thanks for giving our Reader Service a try!*

## THE HARLEQUIN READER SERVICE®: HERE'S HOW IT WORKS

Accepting free books places you under no obligation to buy anything. You may keep the books and gift and return the shipping statement marked "cancel". If you do not cancel, about a month later we will send you 4 additional novels, and bill you just $2.44 each plus 25¢ delivery and applicable sales tax, if any.* That's the complete price, and—compared to cover prices of $3.25 each—quite a bargain! You may cancel at any time, but if you choose to continue, every month we'll send you 4 more books, which you may either purchase at the discount price...or return at our expense and cancel your subscription.

*Terms and prices subject to change without notice. Sales tax applicable in N.Y.

Finally, Travis sent Newt to ride the fence line to the west and sent Harley to the south. With a jubilant shout, they set off hell-for-leather in different directions. Then Travis wheeled Red around, and with a shout of his own, rode southwest, following in Snake's dust.

Snake was in the kitchen when Travis strode in and tossed his hat on the kitchen table. A quick survey of the room revealed no major damage. "Where is she?" he asked, tugging off his gloves.

"She sittin' out in the truck, workin' up the courage to practice her drivin'."

"Oh, Lord," Travis said. "Has she figured out how to start the truck?"

Snake reached in his pocket and tossed the keys at Travis. "She was lookin' for these when I came in. I wouldn't worry about her gettin' far, unless you think she can hot-wire it."

Travis chuckled, tossed the keys in the air, then shoved them in his shirt pocket. "I wouldn't put anything past our princess."

Though he was tempted to go outside and find Josie, he knew he'd probably be talked into giving her another driving lesson. Right now he had some bookwork to do and the payroll to take care of. Besides, knowing Josie and her penchant for trouble, she'd probably find him quick enough.

And she did, thirty minutes later, when she burst in the front door. Travis looked up from his work and watched her as she slammed the door behind her. Breathing hard, she turned around and opened it a crack, then peered out. Her hair, usually fixed in a tidy braid down the middle of her back, had come loose and tangled riotously around her shoulders and face. A smudge of dirt marred her cheek and her backside was dusty.

"You flea-bitten, foul-tempered, four-flushing spawn of Satan," she shouted out the door. "In Jamaica, people eat goats. It wouldn't take much to put you on a plane, you—" The next words that came out of her mouth were colorful enough to make even the most grizzled mule skinner blush. Obviously, Josie had been spending a fair amount of time over the past few weeks with Harley and Newt and, in the process, had picked up a number of their favorite expletives along the way.

"Hard day at the office, dear?" Travis said.

Josie spun around and backed against the door, her eyes wide with surprise. "Travis! I didn't realize you were here."

"I gathered that much. You want to tell me why you're airin' your lungs at Winnie?"

"That damn goat!" Josie cried. "She ate through her rope. I chased her halfway to Deadwater Gulch before she turned around and chased me back. She knocked me down once and ran right over the top of me! You have got to do something about her!"

"What would you suggest I do?" Travis asked.

"I think we should ask Snake to make us a nice Winnie stew," she muttered. "Or maybe I should have just let her run away. At least the coyotes would have had a tasty meal."

Travis stood and crossed the room. He was tempted to wipe the smudge of dirt from her cheek, to dust off her backside and then give her a kiss to make her feel better. Instead he held out an envelope to Josie. "Maybe this will brighten your day."

"Unless it's the bill of sale for that vicious goat, don't count on it." She opened the envelope. "What is this?"

"Your paycheck," he said.

Josie looked, disbelief coloring her sparkling green eyes. "But I thought . . . I mean, I'm still on probation, aren't I?"

"You've been working hard and I think you deserve it. I left the top line blank, since I don't know your last name." Travis waited for her to volunteer the information, but she didn't. "Don't spend it all in one place," he added after a long silence.

Josie stared at the check, then clutched it to her chest and giggled. "Where would I possibly spend it?"

"Well, Harley and Newt usually blow their paychecks at Javelina's, but—"

"If that's where the boys go to relax, then that's where I want to go, too," Josie cried. "After all, I'm working on Castle Creek just like they are, and I want to fit in, so I should do what they do, right?"

Travis frowned and shook his head. "Josie, I don't think Javelina's is a very good place for you to hang out, or to spend your paycheck. It can get a little rough."

She shrugged and pushed away from the door, still staring at her check distractedly. "But I've been there before. They all know me."

"That doesn't make a difference."

Scowling, she looked up at him in confusion. "I don't get it. Why shouldn't I go?"

"Josie, just take my word. It would not be a good idea."

Her spine stiffened and Travis knew what was coming. Josie had a contrary streak wider than Aravaipa Canyon and he had an uncanny knack for bringing it to the surface. He knew how important it was for her to fit in, especially after she'd had such a rough time of it on Castle Creek. But Javelina's was not the place for her to spend her newfound wealth or sharpen her social skills.

"Well, just because you're my boss," she said in a huffy tone, "doesn't mean you can tell me where to spend my paycheck. If I want to go to Javelina's with Newt and Harley, you can't stop me."

"I damn well can!" Travis stated. "I can order Newt and Harley to leave you here."

"Then I'll drive myself," she said.

Travis pulled the keys from his pocket. "Not without these, you won't."

She grabbed for the keys, but Travis held them high above his head. Her breasts rubbed up against his chest as she tried to snatch the keys from his hand and a flood of warmth rushed to his lap. With an extra eight inches on Josie's height, Travis knew she'd never reach what she was after before he reached the end of his self-control.

After an excruciating thirty seconds of body-to-body contact, Josie finally gave up and crossed her arms in front of her, pushing her lower lip out in a pretty pout. "Then I'll ask Snake to take me," she said.

"Snake spends Friday night with his cookbooks and his French tapes."

"You have an answer for everything, don't you?" she said, stamping her foot. "It's my life! I should be able to do what I want without having to ask your permission."

"Josie, look at yourself."

She reached up and touched her cheek, then glanced down at her clothes. "What's wrong with the way I look?"

"Nothing. You're a beautiful woman, the only woman these cowboys have seen in weeks. That, along

with a lot of cheap whiskey, can make for a very...
volatile combination."

This time Josie laughed, her little tantrum forgotten.
"Travis, get real. Look at me. Look at these clothes.
Those cowboys would have to be drunk as skunks, and
blind, to boot, before they found me sexually attractive."

"You don't know what you're talking about, Josie."

"Neither do you," she shot back, tipping her chin up
defiantly and challenging his authority.

Travis grabbed her by the shoulders and stared into
her glittering gaze. "Why do you have to disagree with
everything I say?"

"Why won't you let me go?"

"Because *I* find you sexually attractive, damn it, and
I'm not drunk or blind."

Josie opened her mouth to respond, then frowned
and snapped it shut. She arched her brow skeptically,
then shifted uneasily on her feet. "Then maybe you
should come along. That way you can point out all
these horny cowboys personally."

"Horny?" Travis groaned and raked his fingers
through his hair. "If I say no, you're not going to let up,
are you?"

She shook her head and smiled fetchingly.

"All right," he said. "We'll go and have a few drinks.
And if I see any signs of those cowboys goin' on a tear,
I'll have you out of there in two shakes of a cow's tail."

"Three shakes," she countered playfully.

Travis gave her a reluctant grin. "If I were you, I
wouldn't push your luck."

She stared up at him, waiting for him to acquiesce,
her eyes wide, her expression animated. His senses
sharpened as he felt the warm curves of her shoulders

beneath his hands, smelled the faint scent of his shampoo in her hair. His heart picked up speed and his blood warmed as he fought the temptation to lean forward and kiss her, the need to pull her into his arms and cover her mouth with his.

Instead he marshaled his resolve and released her. He cleared his throat. "You'd better get yourself cleaned up. Snake will have supper ready soon. And I've got some work to do out in the barn for the next half hour."

Travis turned and grabbed his hat from the desk. She'd want to use his bathroom and the only way she'd do it was if he was gone. When he'd first moved to the ranch, an indoor bathroom had been a luxury he could ill afford, but he'd put one in anyway, sinking a major portion of his savings into plumbing fixtures. But now he wondered if the decision hadn't been strangely providential. Though he didn't know it at the time, the bathroom would provide him with more pleasure than he'd ever anticipated.

Travis stifled a smile. Sooner or later he'd have to tell her that he knew about her midnight visits. But until that time he just might want to enjoy the view again . . . when he felt in better control of himself.

"LOOK AT THIS, boys! Our princess is back!"

Travis instinctively scanned the room as he showed Josie through the door of Javelina's. Her adoring subjects cheered and shouted and whistled their welcome and he knew the rowdy group of weather-beaten cowboys had already had too much to drink. As Travis had predicted, she was the only woman in the place.

He glanced around the smoky room, evaluating the crowd. They looked harmless enough, but he'd been in Javelina's more than once when a simple conversation had turned into a fistfight in a matter of seconds. He bent close to her ear. "The first sign of trouble," he warned softly, "and we're out of here."

She turned and gave him a sweet smile. "Don't worry," she said. "I'm a big girl and I can take care of myself."

"That's exactly what I'm afraid of," Travis said. "So just stick close to me."

Though she wore her everyday clothes, she'd chosen to leave her hair long and loose and free of its confining braid. The silky dark strands nearly reached her tiny waist, a waist accentuated by her snug jeans and the flannel shirt she had tied in a knot in the front.

As they made their way through the room, the crowd parted, the cowboys removing their hats as if royalty was passing by. Josie stopped to chat with the boys along the way, and by the time they found a place at the bar, she'd been personally introduced to everyone in the room. She soaked up the adoration as if she'd been born to it and accepted the cowboys' welcome as her due. For the first time since he'd met her, Travis had cause to believe she might just be a real princess.

Harley and Newt hovered over her, protecting her like two well-trained and vigilant bodyguards. If Travis had any concerns about her safety, he hadn't counted on the determination of his two ranch hands. They were as besotted with her as every other cowboy in the room.

"What can I get you, Princess?" Jake asked, polishing the bar in front of her until it shone like glass.

She graced him with a bright smile. "Whiskey," she said. "And buy Newt and Harley a drink...and Travis, too."

"Give her a whiskey and soda," Travis amended. "And I'll have a beer."

Josie fixed Travis with a glare that could have easily bored another tunnel through the Mule Mountains. "I'll have a whiskey and soda," she said, then turned to Jake. "But hold the soda."

Travis ground his teeth. She was purposely testing his patience. His normally agreeable princess was out to prove a point tonight. She'd been prickly toward him ever since the kiss they'd shared on the way back from Bisbee. "Josie, I—"

"Travis," she said, leaning toward him. Her breath felt soft and warm on his cheek. Her flannel shirt gaped open in front and his gaze darted to the soft flesh it revealed. She wasn't wearing any underwear, at least not on top. "Please don't patronize me. I'm an adult and I can do what I like. You have no right to tell me how to live my life. If that causes a problem, then I'd suggest you leave."

Jake set a shot glass in front of her and she picked it up, drew a deep breath, then defiantly downed it in one gulp. She fought hard to maintain her composure, barely holding back the tears as the whiskey burned its way to her stomach. Slamming the shot glass down on the bar, she gave Travis a smug smile. "Good whiskey," she said in a gruff voice.

"Josie, you're testing my patience."

She spun on her bar stool and grabbed Newt by the arm. "And you're acting like my mother," Josie said. "Come on, Newt, let's dance."

Newt's eyes threatened to pop out of his head as she dragged him over to the jukebox. He stumbled over his feet a few times, but was too captivated to inform Josie that he didn't dance. They began a clumsy two-step, every eye in the house fixed on the princess and her maladroit prince.

"She's a feisty little thing, ain't she?" Harley said. "Purdy, too. Don't you think?"

Travis nodded as he watched Newt wrap his arm around Josie's slender waist. Though Newt tried valiantly, the kid had two left feet, and a few seconds later another cowboy cut in and led Josie through the steps of a Western dance.

Over the next hour each cowboy took a turn around the room with her, the others clapping and hooting their approval. For such a domestic klutz, she was a surprisingly graceful dancer. Each new step was studied and quickly repeated after just one demonstration. Travis had the sneaking suspicion that she'd spent more than a few nights dancing the Achy-Breaky and the Boot Scoot with a cowboy on her arm.

From princess to cow bunny, Travis mused. Just who was the real Josephine?

He reached back for his beer and took a long swallow. Strange how this was the first clue he had to her former life. This and the fact that she hated authority. And then there was that cryptic statement about picking with her feet, which he still hadn't figured out yet.

Maybe she had a novelty banjo act . . . in a Western dance hall . . . working for an overbearing boss. Travis closed his eyes and thoroughly cussed himself out. Hell, why did he care? She was his employee and nothing more. Sure, he'd kissed her once. All right, maybe twice. Three times if he counted that first night. But that didn't mean he was falling for her. Come to think of it, he was being pretty damn circumspect considering the fact he hadn't touched a woman in almost a year. And considering the fact that she managed to look so damn irresistible, even when she was covered from head to toe in dust.

All right, so he cared. He cared enough to dream about her at night, to imagine what she'd feel like in his arms, in his bed. But it went beyond that. He cared about her feelings, her happiness, her fears and insecurities. And he was starting to care about her future, too.

Travis glanced up, then slowly set the beer bottle down behind him. And right now, he cared that she was dancing with Chase Mitchell.

There weren't many people Travis mistrusted in the world, but Chase was at the top of the list. He was spoiled and childish and more than a little arrogant, and—Travis's gaze fixed on Josie's flushed face—he was charming the socks right off Travis's very own personal princess.

Travis stood. He'd just have to go over and cut in. Chase Mitchell was not the sort of man he wanted Josie dancing with. Living up to his name, Chase was a notorious ladies' man, though the ladies seemed to do the lion's share of the chasing. The prospect of a lush life on the Mitchell family's very large and very successful ranch was enough to keep Chase in pretty women twelve months out of the year.

But if Travis went over and cut in, she'd just accuse him of trying to run her life. As Harley would say, Josie was as tetchy as a teased snake tonight . . . a teased snake that wasn't wearing her underwear.

He slowly sat down. Why the hell did he care if she danced with Chase Mitchell? Was he really concerned for her safety? After all, she was just another employee.

Then why did he feel an overwhelming flood of jealousy as he watched her in another man's arms? He swore silently, then grabbed his beer and finished it in one long swallow. Yeah, he was jealous, all right.

Travis slammed the bottle down on the bar, then jumped off his bar stool. Josie didn't notice his approach until he tapped Mitchell on the shoulder. To his surprise, Josie smiled at him with obvious relief and attempted to step out of Mitchell's arms and into his. But Chase pulled her tighter against his body, preventing her escape. Travis felt a rush of anger shoot through him.

"I'm cuttin' in, Mitchell," he said in a deceptively even voice.

Chase slowly turned and gave Travis an insolent glare. "Go away, McKinnon. Can't you see I'm entertaining a lady here?"

"I brought the lady and now I'm collecting my dance."

Chase turned back to Josie. "You don't want to dance with this guy, do you, Princess? Haven't you heard the stories?"

Josie forced a smile, her gaze darting between Travis and Chase. "What stories?"

"McKinnon's a damned environmentalist. All those crazy ideas he has about plantin' grass and burnin' brush. He comes here from Chicago thinkin' he's got a new way to ranch. Hell, he oughta be playin' with a string of spools."

"They're not crazy ideas," Josie said defensively.

Travis clamped his hand on Chase's shoulder. "Listen, Mitchell. You've had a little too much to drink, so I'm not going to take what you're saying too serious."

Chase knocked his hand away and pulled Josie back into his arms. "Good," he replied. "Then I won't take you too serious, either. Come on, sweetheart, let's dance."

Josie wriggled around in his embrace. "I'd really like to dance with Travis now," she said, pushing against his chest with her palms.

"Honey, you don't want to dance with him. If he dances the way he ranches, he'll be trippin' all over your toes."

Travis wasn't exactly sure what happened next. He had simply taken a moment to bask in the glow of Josie's quick defense of his ranching strategies when the sound of Josie's palm cracking against Chase Mitchell's cheek told him all was not well. The sound was like a starter's gun at a land rush. An instant later, the bar erupted.

Without an overindulgence in whiskey to hamper his reflexes, Travis deflected most of the punches thrown. But when Chase Mitchell came after him, he couldn't resist throwing one of his own. Mitchell went from vertical to horizontal—and somewhere on the way down acquired himself a bloody nose.

In a matter of seconds each cowboy had chosen a side and joined in. The hands from the Bar M fought on Mitchell's side. To keep the fight even, the rest of the cowboys chose the other side, which would probably be considered Travis's side. And in the middle of it all was Princess Josephine, wielding a deadly looking whiskey bottle.

Josie was about to smash the bottle over Mitchell's head when Travis grabbed her wrist from behind. She balled her free hand into a fist, turned, and swung at him, catching him squarely in the midsection. The air left Travis's lungs in a whoosh and he gasped for his next breath.

He quickly grabbed Josie's other hand before she could land another blow with the bottle, stretching her arms high above her head. It was only then, when she was virtually hog-tied, that she was forced to look up at him. Her eyes went wide with surprise and her expression became instantly apologetic.

"I told you this would happen," Travis growled as the air slowly returned to his lungs. "Come on, we're getting out of here. Now!"

"THIS IS YOUR FAULT, not mine," Josie said, staring out the front window of the truck.

"How is this my fault?" Travis replied.

Josie scrambled to come up with a plausible explanation, but considering all the facts, what had happened was exactly what Travis had predicted. First, he'd tried to tell her what to do, and then he'd had the audacity to be right! Lord, she hated it when he was right.

"You started the fight," she said. "You're the one who came over and tried to cut in like some dime-store John Wayne."

"And you weren't glad to see me? Jeez, Josie, the guy was practically groping you on the dance floor. What did you expect me to do? Besides, you threw the first punch. Cowboy law says you started it."

She glanced over at him. The light from the dashboard bathed his masculine features in soft orange and deep shadow. "I was defending your honor."

"I don't need my honor defended, Josie. Especially not with Chase Mitchell."

"I could have handled him myself," she said. "I was handling him until you came along."

Travis laughed harshly, but his firm mouth showed no trace of a smile. "How? By gazing up at him with those beautiful green eyes of yours? By telling him what a terrific dancer he was? From what I could see, it looked like *he* was in charge of most of the handling," Travis muttered.

"Can we just stop discussing this? You obviously aren't ready to say anything I'd be interested in hearing." She tugged her denim jacket more tightly around her, then slid to the far side of the front seat.

"Fine," he said.

"Fine."

The truck coughed, as if to add its opinion to the matter. Then it coughed again, and sputtered, before it lurched to a stop. Travis reached down and turned the key in the ignition, but the engine answered with a halfhearted groan.

"What's wrong?" Josie asked.

"It won't start."

"I can see that. What's wrong with it?"

Travis shot her an impatient glare. "I don't know. It sounds like it's out of gas."

Josie rolled her eyes and sighed. "Oh, right. This is the oldest trick in the book. You've got me alone, in the middle of nowhere, in a truck without gas, and you have the nerve to question Chase Mitchell's intentions."

"Believe me, I don't need to resort to tricks to get a woman," Travis said.

"Then what do you call this?"

"I'd call it a shortage of fuel in the gas tank."

"Didn't you check it before we left?"

"The gauge is busted."

"So now we're stuck out here in the middle of nowhere?"

Travis leaned back in his seat and tapped his fingers on the steering wheel, as if he were trying very hard to control his temper. "Until Newt and Harley come along. They've got to come home sometime and they have to come this way. We'll just hitch a ride with them."

"I'm not spending another minute in this truck with you." Josie pushed her door open. "I'm walking the rest of the way."

She stood in front of the truck and buttoned her jacket, then looked out at the road ahead. The headlights illuminated only twenty or thirty yards, but the road was two furrows of hard-packed dirt, easy enough to follow, even in the dark.

Travis hit the horn and she jumped. She peered around the side of the truck to find him leaning out his window. "Watch out for the coyotes," he said, a teasing smirk on his face.

She braced her hands on her hips. "I'm not scared of any sorry old coyotes. In fact, I don't believe there are any coyotes around here. You just use the poor creatures to scare me when it suits your purpose."

Josie started down the road, following the beams of the headlights. By the time she reached the end of the light, she had decided that she'd make it back to the ranch house, coyotes be damned.

She heard the truck door slam behind her. "Damn it, Josie," Travis called. "There's at least three miles of desert between here and the house and I'm not letting you walk that alone."

"Try and stop me," she shouted over her shoulder.

"Is that an invitation?"

"It's a warning," Josie replied.

The darkness seemed to swallow her, messing with her equilibrium until the only way she could maintain her balance was to fix her gaze at the point on the horizon where the stars met the black.

She heard his footsteps behind her and smiled—until he grabbed her around the waist, spun her around, and threw her over his shoulder. Josie screamed, the sound echoing in the night.

"Put me down!" She kicked her legs and pummeled his back with her fists, then screamed again. From a distance came an answering cry, a long, low animal howl that seemed to hang in the air around them.

She held her breath and listened. "What was that?" she asked, pushing against his back to peer into the dark.

"Some sorry old coyote, I suspect," Travis replied. "Or maybe it was Chase Mitchell howlin' at the moon."

"Just stop it!" Josie snapped. "If I didn't know better, I'd think you were jealous. Now put me down."

"Well, I'm not," Travis said. He set her back on her feet in front of the truck, pulled his hat off, then braced his hands on either side of her.

"I know that," she said, shoving her shoulder against his arm. "But you *are* controlling and overbearing and stubborn. I don't belong to you, Travis McKinnon. I'm not some horse or cow that will just docilely do whatever you say."

Travis sighed and pressed his body up against her, effectively preventing her escape. She wriggled beneath him, but found that did nothing more than bring him closer. The feel of his body against hers muddled her thoughts and jumbled her senses.

"Who appointed you my protector?" she demanded.

"You did," he said softly. "The minute you set foot on Castle Creek, you became my responsibility. And I don't take my responsibilities lightly."

"Well, you needn't worry about me. As soon as I make enough for bus fare, I'll get out of your hair."

Travis cursed quietly. "That's not what I meant, Josie. You don't have to leave. I—I don't want you to leave."

He raised his hand and splayed his fingers across her cheek, gazing down into her eyes. A current seemed to pass between them, shaking her resolve and slowly transforming anger into desire.

Suddenly her senses seemed more acute, every impression crystallizing in her foggy mind. She saw his quickened breath as each exhale frosted in the night air. She smelled the spicy masculine scent of his clothes and felt the worn canvas of his jacket clutched in her own fingers.

His body, long and lean, molded against hers, and she could feel the hard muscle and strong sinew beneath his clothes. She pressed herself closer and the proof of his desire branded her belly through the fabric of his jeans. She had no choice anymore. A force, so much greater than she was able to resist, had splintered her control.

Slowly he lowered his head and touched her lips with his. A tremor of passion raced through her the instant his mouth covered hers, a quake that rocked her to her very core. He pressed her back against the hood of the truck and Josie pulled her leg up against his thigh, wanting, needing him to come closer.

"We shouldn't do this," she murmured. "You're my boss. I'm your employee."

"Hell, I don't feel much like your boss right now, Josie." He teased at her lower lip with his teeth. "And you don't feel much like an employee."

She slipped her arms around his neck and returned his kiss in full measure. Lord, she wanted him, right here, in the middle of the desert under the stars. This was what she had wanted all along, from the moment she'd looked down on him as he'd slept that first night. And no matter how much she'd fought it these last few weeks, she couldn't fight it anymore.

In all her life she'd never wanted to open her heart to another person. She had fiercely protected it, knowing that an unkind word or a disappointed look might be all it finally took to shatter her soul into a million pieces. But then she'd come to Castle Creek and the ice that had encased her heart had slowly begun to melt, warmed by the desert sun and Travis McKinnon's easy smile.

He buried his face in the curve of her neck. "I'm sorry about earlier," Travis murmured. "I didn't mean to make you angry."

"It's not your fault," she replied, raining a trail of tiny kisses along his jawline. "It's just that all my life people have told me what to do and when to do it."

"And I was doing the same thing," he said.

She nodded, running her fingers through his hair. "I always did exactly as I was told. And then one day I realized that I hadn't been living my life, I'd been living someone else's life. I don't know whose it was, but it wasn't mine."

"Is that why you ran away?" he whispered.

She pulled back and looked into his eyes. "I'm not running from anything," she said. "Not anymore. I want you to believe that."

"And what else do you want from me, Josie?" he murmured, brushing his lips against hers. "Tell me. Tell me what you want."

His words were laced with need, a need that had become overwhelming in its intensity.

"I—I want you," she murmured.

He slowly unbuttoned her denim jacket. "Do you want me to touch you?" He didn't wait for an answer, but skimmed his palms along her rib cage until they cupped her breasts through the flannel shirt.

"Mmm," she breathed. How long had it been since she'd been touched by a man? So long, yet she knew these feelings had never been as powerful with anyone else. Only Travis had the ability to set her blood aflame until it raced through her veins like wildfire.

"You're not wearing any underwear," he said, rubbing at the hard nubs of her nipples through the flannel shirt.

"And you're beginning to sound like my mother again," she teased.

He opened the front of her shirt one button at a time then parted it just enough to kiss between her breasts. "Heaven forbid," he whispered.

She sucked in a sharp breath as the cold night air hit her hot skin. A shiver ran down her spine. Slowly, with exquisite attention to each inch of flesh he encountered, Travis nuzzled the side of her breast, pushing the flannel away as he moved.

Through her hazy passion, Josie heard a horn beep in the distance but the sound was swallowed up by the beat of her heart and Travis's soft moan. The sound came again, this time closer, and Travis froze, his warm mouth hovering over her puckered nipple. He clasped her hips to his, then picked her up off the truck and peered around the side. A softly muttered oath escaped his lips and he reluctantly unwrapped Josie's legs from around his waist.

"Looks like our ride is here," he muttered. With fumbling fingers, he quickly buttoned up her shirt and straightened her jacket. Josie looked up as his hands moved to close his own shirt, suddenly aware that she had worked the buttons open herself. He reached down and zipped up his jacket, his desire still evident through the faded fabric of his jeans. By the time he put his hat back on, a truck had pulled up beside Travis's pickup.

He cleared his throat. "Howdy, boys," he called.

Harley hung his arm out the open window. "Hey there, boss. You okay?"

Travis nodded. "Something's wrong with the truck. You want to give us a lift home?"

Harley jumped out of the truck and helped Josie inside. She waited for Travis to join her, but he didn't. "You can drive, Harley," Travis said. "I'll ride in the back. I could use the fresh air."

"Too much to drink tonight?" Harley asked.

Josie watched him walk to the back of the truck, then leaned back in the seat and closed her eyes.

"Yeah," she heard Travis call. "I guess that's it."

# 7

THE LATE AFTERNOON light streamed through the gaps between the weathered boards, turning the straw that littered the shed floor into luminous gold. Josie swung the pitchfork over her shoulder, then made her way back to Winnie's stall. The goat was waiting patiently for her when she arrived, but Josie didn't set to cleaning her stall immediately. Instead she plopped down on a bale of hay and cupped her chin in her hand, studying the goat intently.

"We have to talk," she said. "I know you can't answer me, you're a goat. But that's probably for the best, because I'm not sure I'd want to hear what you might have to say. But you are the only other female on this ranch, and I have to talk to someone."

Winnie looked up at her with huge, liquid brown eyes ringed with long lashes. For once she wasn't eating and Josie felt as if the goat was willing to listen.

"You see, everything has been going along quite well," Josie explained. "I mean, between Travis and me. And then something happened last night, something that neither one of us expected. We almost . . . well, we let passion get the better of us."

Josie ran her fingers through her hair and shook her head. "I can't believe I'm telling this to a goat." Taking a deep breath, she continued. "I just didn't expect to feel such…" She searched for the word. "Desire. And when we got back to the ranch I thought we'd just continue on from where we left off."

Winnie shook her head, jangling the bell around her neck, then bleated softly.

"I know. Pretty stupid, huh? But we were alone in the house and I thought for sure we'd end up in bed together. We had barely walked in the door and he had to go fix the truck. He ran out of the house like the place was on fire. And it was nearly midnight. And when I got up this morning, he was gone. I think he's avoiding me and I'm not sure why."

She looked at Winnie for some explanation, but the goat was now prancing nervously around the stall.

"It's not that I expect a future with him. I know I have to make a life for myself first before I can make a life with someone else. And I know he doesn't want a future with me. But that doesn't mean we couldn't have a . . . brief liaison. I think he finds me sexually attractive, don't you? I mean, if he didn't, why would he have kissed me that way?"

The goat answered her with a mournful "baa" then collapsed at Josie's feet. For extra emphasis Winnie rolled over onto her side and began to pant heavily.

"I know, I know. The thought of having sex with Travis McKinnon is a little overwhelming to me, too. But I think it would be really good." She paused. "Really, *really* good. Better than good—it would probably be great."

She glanced down at Winnie, but this time the goat didn't respond. In fact, with her tongue hanging out the side of her mouth, Winnie looked downright ill. Josie knelt beside her and peered into the goat's eyes. "What's wrong? You aren't sick, are you?"

A long moan rumbled in the goat's chest. Josie jumped to her feet, staring down at Winnie uneasily. "You *are* sick." She put her hand on the goat's forehead. "You don't feel like you have a fever . . . but then, I don't know what's considered normal for a goat. Don't worry. I'll find Snake." She patted Winnie on the neck reassuringly. "Just relax. Everything will be all right. Maybe it's just the flu."

Josie backed out of the stall, watching Winnie the whole while. It didn't look like the flu. It looked worse, as though Winnie were in desperate pain. She tried the ranch house first and when she didn't find Snake there, she headed for the bunkhouse. A search of the one-room building proved fruitless, as did a quick survey of all the outbuildings. As a last resort she stood in the middle of the yard and shouted Snake's name for five minutes before she accepted the fact that she was entirely alone, in the middle of nowhere, without a doctor in sight.

She had no idea what to do. She'd never dealt with a sick goat before. But Winnie was her responsibility and if something happened to her, she'd never forgive herself. A veterinarian would be the first person to call, but the phone company hadn't run a line out to Cattle Creek yet. The closest phone was at Javelina's. She could get there, but didn't even know who to call once she did.

Josie closed her eyes and tried to collect herself. Snake had told her that Travis and the boys had set out at dawn to repair the fence line to the southwest. If she took the truck and drove south from the ranch house until she hit the fence line, then drove west, logic told her that she'd find him.

But she'd only driven the truck once. And she'd never started it, though she'd seen Travis start the pickup a number of times. An image of Winnie, her trusting eyes looking up at Josie, flashed through her mind. Gathering her confidence, she quickly retrieved the keys from the house, scribbled a quick note to Snake, then climbed in the truck.

Josie pushed the key into the ignition and turned it, saying a silent prayer to the patron saint of healthy goats. A triumphant shout burst from her lips when the engine sprang to life. Setting off toward the south, she followed a pair of bumpy dirt ruts as far as she could, then came to a gate in the barbed-wire fence.

After she passed through the gate and closed it behind her, the road became even harder to distinguish from the desert around her. She stared through the dust-coated windshield, sure that she'd have to reach another fence line before long. She'd been driving nearly thirty minutes and had almost given up hope when she spied a barbed-wire fence in the distance.

Pressing down on the accelerator, she bumped along at a speedy five miles an hour, certain that she'd find Travis soon. The gully seemed to appear out of nowhere, one moment blending in with the colorless desert and the next, gaping in front of the truck. She moved to slam on the brake, but instead hit the gas pedal, sending the truck, nose first, into the deep gully. The impact of the stop threw her body forward.

Stars appeared before Josie's eyes and she reached up to touch her head where it had bumped the steering wheel. Her fingers came back dotted with blood. She glanced in the rearview mirror. A knot had sprung up on her forehead and she winced as she pressed her fingers on the cut to staunch the bleeding.

When her forehead finally stopped bleeding and her body stopped trembling, she gripped the steering wheel with white-knuckled hands. She pressed on the accelerator, but the truck didn't move. She wasn't quite sure how to put it in reverse, but if "P" stood for Park and "D" for Drive, she assumed "R" had to be for Reverse. She shifted the truck and pressed down on the gas pedal again, but still the truck wouldn't budge.

"No," she cried. "I can't be stuck."

Josie scrambled out of the truck and peered beneath it. Though she didn't know much about automotive matters, she could tell that the pickup wasn't going anywhere. The front bumper was jammed up under the bank of the creek bed and the back wheels were on impossibly steep ground.

She leaned back on the rear bumper of the truck and rubbed her head. What was she supposed to do now? She couldn't possibly push the truck out on her own. Walking seemed to be the only answer. But which way? Toward where she thought Travis might be or back to where she knew the ranch house was?

Josie pinched her eyes shut and tried to gather her scrambled thoughts. She should wait with the truck. Someone would notice sooner or later that she was gone and then they'd come looking for her. She gazed at the western sky. The sun would be down in a few hours. If she decided to walk, she'd have to start now and pray that she'd find her way before darkness fell.

In the end, she decided to stay with the truck. The sun was just dipping below the horizon when she spotted a figure outlined against the blazing pink sky—a man leading a horse, a tall, slender figure with an easy, athletic gait that she recognized immediately.

Josie scrambled out of the truck and ran toward Travis. When she reached him, she threw her arms around his neck. "Thank God, I found you," she cried breathlessly. "There's something wrong with Winnie. You have to come back to the ranch with me."

He pulled back and touched her forehead gently. "What happened? Are you all right?"

"I bumped my head. But don't worry about that. Worry about poor Winnie. She's sick. I—I think she might be dying." She pulled him toward the truck and he took in the scene, his brow furrowed in confusion.

Travis peered around her. "What happened to the truck? Is that how you hit your head?" He grabbed her chin and stared at the knot on her forehead. "Are you sure you're okay? Are you dizzy?"

"Travis, you don't seem to be listening. We have to get back to the ranch right away. Winnie is ill. She's lying on her side and she's panting. And she looks like she's in pain. I—I think she might be . . . dying."

He pressed Red's reins into her hands and bent down to examine the truck. "Josie, Winnie is not sick. She's going to have a kid." Dropping down to his knees, he looked beneath the truck. "How the hell did the truck end up stuck like this?"

"A kid?" Josie asked, momentarily stunned.

"Winnie is going to have a baby goat. In fact, she was supposed to have her kid over a month ago. I took her to the vet the same day I drove into Tucson and you hopped in the back of the trailer with her. You must have seen the creek bed. Didn't you at least try to stop?"

"But, I didn't even know she was pregnant," Josie murmured. "Why didn't you tell me? And just where is the father?"

"The father lives at another ranch," Travis said. "I took Winnie over there to breed her, then brought her home. But forget about that goat!"

"I can't believe she's having this baby alone."

Travis groaned. "Winnie has had three kids on her own before. I'm sure she'll do just fine." He stepped around her to climb into the truck.

Josie watched him through the driver's side window. "What if she needs help?"

"Snake will take care of her. Now, move back." He started the truck and put it into gear, then gunned the engine.

"It's not going to move," Josie said. "I've been trying to get it out for the past two hours."

"I can see that." Travis hopped out of the truck and slammed the door, then circled the truck again, examining the situation more closely.

"We can ride Red back to the ranch," Josie said, "and help Winnie."

Travis appeared from behind the far side of the truck. "Red pulled up lame while we were riding fence, so we can't ride him. I sent Newt and Harley back to the house while I walked him back."

"Well, then we better start walking now. I can't let Winnie go through this alone."

Travis glanced at the horizon. "It's at least a three-hour walk and it's getting dark. And you don't have a jacket. It gets mighty cold out here once the sun goes down."

"But you were going to walk back."

"I was going to go as far as Red would and then I was going to build a fire and bed down for the night."

Josie shivered and rubbed her arms. "I can do that." She felt the sudden need to prove her point, to show him that she wasn't afraid to face the challenge of sleeping outdoors. After all, how hard could it be? If Travis could do it, so could she.

Travis grabbed his jacket from the back of his saddle and helped her into it, then began to unhitch the saddle from Red's back. "There's a line cabin just over that rise back there. It's got an old wood stove and we stock it with canned supplies. We'll spend the night there."

"We're going to spend the night in a cabin?" Josie asked. Somehow the prospect seemed much more unnerving than she would have expected. They spent every night together in the same house, so what was the difference? If something was going to happen between them, it would happen either way. And isn't that what she wanted?

"I'm going to leave my saddle in the truck. If the boys ride out to find you, they'll see the saddle and know where we are. If they don't come, we'll walk back in the morning."

Suddenly she felt a flood of apprehension wash over her. Was she really sure she could handle a night of passion with Travis McKinnon? Or was she merely deluding herself? "Does this . . . this cabin have a bed?" Josie asked.

Travis looked down at her and frowned in confusion. "It's got a small cot. It won't be much different from what you're used to sleeping on."

He grabbed Red's reins from her hands and started off in the direction of the line cabin. Josie stared after him, her eyes wide. Maybe it wouldn't be much different to him. But this attraction between them had to be faced sooner or later, and sooner was good enough for her.

She marshaled her resolve and followed Travis. She was an adult and in charge of her life. If she wanted something to happen, then she would make it happen. And right now, she wanted Travis McKinnon.

The problem was, she wasn't quite sure what she'd do with him once she got him.

SPARKS SCATTERED across the rough plank floor as Travis tossed another log into the cast-iron wood stove. A pan of baked beans and canned sausages bubbled on top of the stove and a kerosene lantern sputtered on the scarred wood table, the soft light wavering with every icy draft that slipped through the cracks in the walls.

Travis glanced over at Josie. Oh, Lord, this was a mistake, pure and simple. He should have risked pneumonia and coyotes and getting lost in the low desert. But instead he had brushed off all his misgivings about spending time alone with her and brought her here—where they were undisputably and incontrovertibly alone.

He couldn't deny the attraction any longer. He wanted Josie, more than he could ever remember wanting another woman in his life. His fingers itched to touch her soft skin and his mind whirled with fleeting images of what they might share together.

She watched him from the narrow cot, her feet tucked under her, an old blanket wrapped around her shoulders. She had unbraided her hair and it flowed softly over her shoulders, catching the light from the lantern until, as if he were looking straight into the sun, his eyes just couldn't take it any longer. He turned back to the fire and stared into the flames instead.

"Do you stay here often?" she asked.

"When we're working out here, we do," Travis replied. "The cabin's been here since right after the turn of the century. Castle Creek is just outside the back door, or what's left of it. It's just a dry creek bed now. In fact, it's the same creek bed you ran the truck into."

She frowned, then stood and began to wander around the room. He watched her out of the corner of his eye as she circled around him. She stopped and stared up at the rough-hewn timber above the door, then reached up and traced her fingers along the carved letters. "'J.M. loves N.M.,'" she read.

"Jack McKinnon loves Nell McKinnon. This is the house that my grandfather and grandmother lived in when they first came to Castle Creek. My dad and his two sisters were born right in this very room."

"It must have been a hard life," she said.

"It was the middle of the Depression when they moved here. Castle Creek was a hell of place to bring a new bride."

"If they loved each other, maybe it wasn't so bad," Josie said softly, turning to watch him astutely.

He shook his head. "Don't attach any romantic notions to it. Life on this ranch is hard now. It was much harder back then. This is no place for a woman."

A long silence hung between them, the crackle of the fire and the wail of the wind the only sounds to permeate the cabin. Travis fed another log to the fire.

He heard her draw a deep breath, then groan. "All right, just say it. Go ahead. I know you want to."

Travis stood and brushed his hands on his thighs. He turned and risked a glance in her direction. Lord, she was gorgeous, looking at him with huge green eyes and that hurt expression on her face, her hair all tumbled down around her face. "Say what?"

"You're fired. That's what you want to say. Ever since I came here, you've wanted me to leave, so here's your chance."

His jaw tightened. "That's not what I want to say."

"I can do this job!" she cried.

"Did I say you couldn't?"

"I know what you're thinking. You're thinking that I make a mess of everything that I try. But I can make this work. I have to. And all this talk about Castle Creek not being a fit place for a woman isn't going to change my mind."

Travis picked up the pan of beans and sausages, dumped it onto two tin plates and slid the plates onto the table. He scrounged up a pair of forks, then pulled out a chair and sat down. "Dinner's ready. Come and get it."

Josie wandered over and found a place at the table. She didn't eat, merely picked at her food in silence.

He drew a deep breath and asked a question that had been plaguing his mind ever since he'd kissed her in the desert night. "How long do you plan to hide out on Castle Creek?"

She looked up at him, her eyes wide, her perfect teeth worrying at her lower lip.

"Josie, whatever you're running from, you can't hide here forever. I haven't asked any questions, but I'm thinking that maybe I should have. At least you'd be forced to face your problems."

She sighed and pushed her plate away. "All right. You want to know about my life, I'll tell you. Ask me a question and I'll answer. But for every question you ask, I get to ask one, too."

Travis scooped up a forkful of beans and chewed slowly, contemplating the opportunity to learn more about the woman who invaded his dreams. "What's your name?" he finally asked. "Your real name."

She tipped her chin up defiantly and tugged the blanket tighter around her shoulders. "Josephine Marie Eastman. Now it's my turn. Why do you have such a negative attitude about women? Is it because your ex-fiancée walked out on you?"

"That's two questions. How do you know about her?"

"Newt and Harley told me," Josie explained. "And you can't answer a question with a question. Do you have such a bad attitude about women because your ex-fiancée ran out on you?"

"I don't have a negative attitude. And she didn't run out, she decided that ranch life wasn't for her, that's all."

"Do you still love her?" Josie asked softly.

Travis raised his brow and stared at her apprehensive expression. "It's my turn now. Where are you from?"

"Out east," Josie replied.

"That's not an acceptable answer. Be more specific."

"Fairfield, Connecticut. Is that specific enough for you?"

"Yes. Now, tell me what you're running from."

"What about my question?"

"What are you running from?" he repeated. "Tell me, Josie. I need to know."

She pushed away from the table and paced the room, glancing over at him every now and then. "I'm not running away," she said imploringly. "Not anymore. I had been running away from responsibility my whole life, but now I'm in charge. I'm making decisions for myself. And everything that's happened in my life before I came to Castle Creek doesn't make a difference to me."

"It makes a difference to me," Travis said.

"Why?" Josie snapped. "Does it make me a different person? Will it make you like me less?"

Travis bit back a curse and stood. He crossed the room and grabbed her by the shoulders, stilling her restless pacing. "Why can't you tell me?" he asked, punctuating each word impatiently.

She closed her eyes and drew a long breath, then looked up at him. "I—I don't want you to know that person. I'm not proud of her. I want you to know me the way I am now." She placed her palm on her chest. "This is the real me, Travis. What you see is what you get. If you don't like it, that's too bad."

He sighed and shook his head in frustration. "I like it," he said softly. "I like it."

Josie stared up at him, then slowly ran her hands along his chest. Pushing up on her tiptoes, she closed her eyes and pressed her lips to his. He refused to yield, refused to respond. She opened her eyes and he saw hurt and confusion color their green depths.

"This is not a good place to start something," Travis said.

Josie frowned. "I—I don't understand. I—I thought you might want . . ." Her voice trailed off, right along with her courage.

"Maybe you should lie down and get some sleep." He steered her toward the cot and covered her with a blanket after she lay down. His gaze locked with hers for a long moment and regret shot through him. "It's not that I don't want to, Josie, because I do. I want to more than you know."

"Is it because I won't tell you about my past?"

He shook his head and chuckled ironically. If it was only that simple. At least he'd have an answer for her. But he didn't know why he couldn't make love to her. Maybe it was a matter of trust, or maybe it was a matter of self-preservation. "I'm just not sure what's beneath all this, Josie. And I'm not sure I want to find out, either."

"Aren't you even the least bit . . . curious about how it would be between us?"

"I know how it will be, Josie. Once we start, we're not going to stop, not for a very long time."

"So why not now? We're here, alone, together. Is . . . is it because you don't find me attractive?"

Travis let out a long, tightly held breath and turned away from her. "Go to sleep, Josie."

"Tell me why," she insisted.

He glanced over his shoulder and blurted the only logical excuse he could make. "Right now, the only thing standing between you and me is a vital piece of . . . protection. Like I said, if we start, I'm not going to stop. If I were you, I'd go to sleep. Now."

He felt her gaze on him as he spread his bedroll on the floor in front of the stove. Stretching out on the thin foam pad, he closed his eyes and tried to forget that she was only a few feet away. But he couldn't banish the image of her from his mind, above him, beneath him, around him. Yet there was something more to these fantasies than just simple gratification. If it were just gratification, he'd be able to accept her offer with no guilt, no hesitation.

Travis threw his arm over his eyes. He didn't want to admit it, but he was falling in love with Josephine Marie Eastman, a woman he knew nothing about. Nothing except that she stirred feelings deep inside of him, feelings he'd never felt before, even with the woman he'd once intended to marry.

"It's freezing in here," Josie murmured. "There's a hole in the wall and the wind is blowing right into my ear."

"Go to sleep, Josie."

"I can't."

With a silent curse, Travis levered himself up and walked over to the bed. "Get up."

She wrapped the blanket around her shoulders and crawled off the cot. He grabbed the edge of the mattress and dragged it across the floor, flopping it down in front of the stove.

Josie laid down and carefully arranged the blanket around her. "This is much better. I think I'll be able to sleep now." She closed her eyes.

"At least one of us will," Travis muttered.

He watched her for a long time, lying on his side, his head braced on his arm. He listened as her breathing grew deep and slow and even. When she finally slept, he reached out and ran his finger along her cheek. "What is it about you, Princess?" he whispered. "Why can't I put you out of my mind?" He fought the temptation to kiss her then, knowing that if she responded he'd be lost.

He was still awake when she wiggled off her mattress and tucked herself into the curve of his body, sighing contentedly, yet still asleep. He hesitantly wrapped his arms around her and pulled her against him, fighting the warm flood of desire that pooled in his lap. Her hair smelled sweet and he buried his face in the soft strands, inhaling deeply and trying to memorize her scent.

She felt right, curled up in his arms, as if they were made to sleep together. He drew another deep breath. What would it be like to fall asleep with her next to him, to wake up to her every morning and watch the sunrise illuminate her delicate features? His mind wandered to bedroom activities beyond sleeping and he allowed himself the fantasies. In the midst of these thoughts, he drifted to sleep.

Travis awoke just as the sun was turning the sky a pale gray and he watched as the light slowly illuminated her features. She was more beautiful than he'd ever imagined she could be, her hair tumbled around her face, her expression sweet and peaceful.

With a long sigh, he disentangled himself from her, pulled the blanket up around her shoulders, then stood. The stove was barely warm and his breath frosted in the chilly air inside the cabin.

He tugged his jacket on and grabbed the ax from beside the door. Splitting wood in the cold morning air would be a lot safer than lying next to Josie as she woke up. After a night of lying beside her, he wasn't sure he had any willpower left at all and he wasn't about to put himself to the test. There would be plenty of opportunities for that in the future.

"AND THIS here's your bed."

Newt stepped aside and indicated a small iron bed tucked into the far corner of the bunkhouse.

Josie smiled distractedly and glanced around the room that was now her home. Each of the four corners boasted a bed and chest of drawers. A potbellied stove sat in the center of the room, surrounded by four well-worn rocking chairs.

She had decided to move her meager possessions into the bunkhouse after she and Travis returned from the line cabin. As soon as they'd reached the house, Travis had deserted her for the barn to work on Red's hoof. Minutes later, he'd saddled another horse and ridden off, making it abundantly clear that he could barely stand to be within a hundred yards of her. Maybe it was for the best, though. She could barely face him after making such a fool of herself.

What had ever possessed her to think she might be able to seduce him?

"We got you a washbowl and pitcher," Newt explained. "You can heat water on the stove and when you want to clean up, you jest have to tell us to leave. We usually wash in the horse trough, but that ain't right for a lady like Yer Highness."

"You don't have to call me that, Newt. Since we're going to be living together, you can call me Josie."

A flood of color rose in Newt's cheeks. "All right, Miss Josie."

"We strung a rope across the corner," Harley said. "We'll hang a blanket so's you can have some privacy. We're all gentlemen here."

"And if you'd prefer a bath, we got an old tub in the lean-to. We'd all be glad to haul water for you. It's real private in there, so's you wouldn't have to worry about us seein' you . . ." Newt's voice drifted off and his face flushed red again at the thought he was about to express.

"Thank you," Josie said. "I appreciate that."

"If you don't mind me askin', why'd you decide to move out of the big house? We thought you and Travis was . . . well, we thought . . ." The color in Newt's cheeks intensified.

"Shut yer trap, Newton," Harley muttered.

"Well, we did," Newt cried. "That's why we left 'em out at the line cabin after we come across the truck, ain't it? So they could have an evenin' of romance, isn't that what you said?"

"You what?" Josie asked.

Harley glared at Newt impatiently. "Boy, you got a big mouth. I told you that was gonna be our secret."

"You didn't tell me any such thing," Newt replied.

"Tell me the truth, boys," Josie ordered.

Harley sighed. "Well, as soon as we got back to the ranch house that night, we saw the truck was gone. We found yer note, so me and Newt set off to rescue you. When we came upon the pickup, we was scared you'd tried to walk back on yer own, but then we seen Travis's saddle and we knew you was safe. So rather than bother you, we figgered we'd just leave you out there so Travis could . . . well, do some sage hennin'."

"Sage henning?" Josie asked.

"Courtin'," Harley explained.

Josie smiled. "I know your intentions were good, but I don't think Travis is interested in courting me."

Newt frowned. "Well, if he ain't interested, can I declare my intentions?" he asked. Harley jabbed his elbow into Newt's side and Newt drew back his fist. "You do that once more, Harley Carson, and I'll knock yer ears down."

"You yack-headed younker," Harley said, slapping Newt on the side of the head. "You got to be off yer mental reservation to think the princess would let you drop yer rope on her."

"You jest want her for yerself!" Newt cried.

Josie put her hands between the two and pushed them apart. "Boys, please don't argue. If my moving out here

is going to cause bad feelings between the two of you,
I'll—"

"No, ma'am," Harley said, slipping his arm around
Newt's shoulders.

"We lock horns all the time and it ain't nothin'," Newt
explained.

"Well, don't lock horns over me, all right?"

"Then you do favor Travis?" Newt asked.

Josie flopped down on the cot and ran her fingers
through her hair. "I don't know. What difference does
it make? He doesn't favor me. And can you blame him?
Everything I touch turns into a disaster."

"Don't say that, Princess," Harley said. "You're doin'
yer best."

"My best." Josie laughed dryly. "If I don't get my act
together soon, he's going to fire me."

"He won't fire you," Harley said.

"How do you know?"

Harley shrugged. "I 'spect Travis is in love with you.
He's jest too bull-necked to see it."

Josie blinked hard. "I—I think you have it wrong,
Harley."

"Nah," Newt replied. "Harley knows Travis pretty
well, almost as well as Snake. If Harley says Travis loves
you, then he loves you."

"See, Travis was caught short when that gal he
brought here from Chicago went runnin' back home,"
Harley explained. "He throwed himself into his work
like a man gone mad. He worked from sunrise till sunset, harder than all us hands put together. I think he was
tryin' to drive that woman from his mind. And then you
came along and he started smilin' again."

"Are you sure that wasn't a grimace on his face?"

"You jest wait. Give the boy some time and he'll come 'round," Harley advised.

"I might not be around to see it," Josie said. "After what I did to his truck, I don't think he's too happy with me." She paused. "The only way I'm going to stay here on Castle Creek is if I can prove to Travis that I'm useful." She glanced up to find Newt *and* Harley flushing a deep red. "I mean, on the ranch . . . working." She shook her head. "You know what I mean."

"You *are* useful," Newt offered.

"But not at what's important, like riding the fence lines and herding the cattle."

"That's not ladies' work," Newt said stubbornly.

"Don't be such a chauvinist!" she cried. "What makes you think I couldn't handle the work?"

"Well, you cain't ride, fer one," he replied softly, his brow furrowed. Newt was obviously contemplating the meaning of the word "chauvinist," not sure whether he'd been insulted or not.

"That don't mean she cain't learn how," Harley said. "Plenty of women work ranches."

Josie clasped her hands to her chest excitedly. "Do you really think I could learn to ride?"

"You could do jest about anything," Newt breathed, his gaze fixed on hers.

"I'll teach you," Harley said.

"And I'll help," Newt added.

Josie smiled in relief. Maybe that's just what she needed to prove that she belonged on Castle Creek. She'd learn to ride and make herself more valuable as an employee. Then Travis wouldn't fire her. After all, she needed this job, at least until she decided it was time to venture out on her own.

But was it really the job she needed? Or was it Travis McKinnon? Lately, the more she tried to convince herself that her time at Castle Creek was just a temporary thing, the more she started to think it might be something more.

Something that she wanted to last.

# 8

TRAVIS SWUNG his leg over Red's back and jumped to the ground, then flipped the horse's reins around the hitching rail in the middle of the yard. He pulled off his hat and dunked his head in the horse trough, washing away a day's worth of dust. He'd been out on the range since sunup, spending most of his time just observing the herd and trying to keep his mind off Josie. She'd moved out of the ranch house three days ago and, since then, he hadn't seen much of her.

A shout from the direction of the corral caught his attention and he turned to see Snake, Harley and Newt. They stared into the corral, their folded arms resting on top of the gate. It was late afternoon, so it wasn't unusual for the trio to be back at the ranch house. What *was* unusual was their standing around with nothing better to do than stare at the horses.

"Gentle now," Snake called. "Just a little tug and she'll turn."

"Don't sit in the saddle," Harley added. "Sit above it. Use your legs."

Newt just stared into the corral with an awestruck expression, his hat pushed way back on his head to afford a better view.

Travis strode across the yard, wiping his face with his bandanna. He came to a stop just behind the boys. As soon as he got there, he saw what had captured their attention so thoroughly. The corral was empty of horses, except for one—a dappled gray mare that Snake preferred. And on top of that mare sat Josephine Eastman, her unbound hair flying out behind her in the stiff breeze, her face furrowed in concentration.

His breath died in his throat as he took in the sight. She sat in the saddle, straight and assured, showing absolutely no fear. Gently nudging the mare with her heels, she set the horse into a walk, then clucked her tongue and slapped the reins to increase her speed to a trot. For a novice rider she was incredibly good, picking up the movement of the horse and adjusting her rhythm accordingly, holding herself just above the saddle with her legs.

Her hat had blown off and now bounced against her back. Travis let his gaze drift along her body as she circled the corral, along the gentle curve of her spine to her shapely backside to her firm legs. As he watched her body rock with the horse's gait, his mind wandered in other directions.

A slow frisson of desire stole through him as an unbidden image of her flashed in his mind. She no longer rode the horse—but sat with her legs straddling Travis's hips, her hands braced on his chest. She moved above him in a gentle, but powerful rhythm. Around them, her long hair formed a curtain as she bent over to kiss him, to murmur her need into his ear. And then her pace became more urgent. She tipped her head back, giving him a view of her heat-flushed body. Faster and faster she moved, until—

Travis drew a sharp breath and drove the image from his mind before it reached completion. He blinked and then turned away from the scene in front of him, rubbing his face with his hands. He was going mad, that was the only explanation.

Since she'd moved out, he'd fallen into an almost total obsession with her. They saw each other only at
meals, for there was nothing else to draw her into the
house when he was at home. But he thought about her
nearly every minute of every waking day. And when
he wasn't awake, he dreamed about her, dreams that
would end in frustration and a cold shower.

She'd settled into her domestic duties at the ranch
without any further disasters, but always set about her
work after he'd left in the morning. When he did stop
in for lunch, she was curiously absent, occupied with
some important chore, and he was forced to look at
Snake across the table.

At breakfast and supper, she paid more attention to
the boys than she did to him. Her new home in the
bunkhouse had provided an opportunity for new
friendships, and the gentle teasing that went on between his four employees was enough to set his teeth on
edge. He was jealous, plain and simple, and he had a
perfect right to be. He'd never had to share his princess
before and he didn't like doing it now.

She'd even stopped her midnight visits to his bathroom, preferring instead to wash up in the bunkhouse.
He'd seen the three hands hauling buckets of water from
the horse trough every night after dinner and been
tempted to ask one of the boys the procedure for her
bath—did they just plop the old copper tub in the middle of the bunkhouse and watch?

Travis stepped up to the fence. "You boys mind telling me what you're doing?"

"Hey there, Travis," Harley said. "We're teaching the
princess to ride. We figured if she was going to be staying on here at the ranch, she should learn how to ride."

"Didn't I ask you boys to fix the tractor so we could pull my pickup out of that gully?"

Harley nodded. "Tractor's all ready to go," he said.

"Then why don't you and Newt get out there and get it done today, instead of standing around here making eyes at the princess."

Harley glanced at Newt, then at Snake. "But it's almost dinnertime," he said.

"We'll wait dinner for you," Travis said.

The pair climbed down from the gate and shuffled off in the direction of the shed, a dispirited slump to their shoulders.

"You plannin' a trip into town?" Snake asked.

Travis's gaze followed the princess as she circled the corral at a trot. "No," he said.

"The truck could have waited until tomorrow, then," Snake commented blandly.

Travis turned and stared at him, his jaw tight. "It's been out there for three days now. I would like to get it fixed before too long."

Snake shrugged. "Yer the boss."

"What's that supposed to mean?"

"It means that you should be happy we're teachin' Josie how to ride. She'll be more use to you around the ranch."

"That's if she stays," Travis muttered.

"Well, I s'pose that's pretty much up to you now, ain't it?" Snake said. "Me and the boys were pretty sure she'd be stayin' after you two spent the night together out at the line cabin, but now we're not so sure."

"Well, don't assume. Nothing happened that night."

"We know," Snake said. "The princess told us."

"What?" Travis gasped. "She told you about that night?"

"We live in the bunkhouse together. We do a lot of talkin' late at night." Snake paused. "You know, it wouldn't be the end of the world if you decided to marry her."

"Marry her?" Travis shook his head. "I'm not planning to marry her. This ranch is no place for a woman. I think my former fiancée proved that point quite well."

"Josie ain't Elaine."

"How do you know? She hasn't even been here a month yet."

"You oughta give her a chance. I think she likes livin' on Castle Creek. She's tryin' awful hard to fit in here."

"She's got no place else to go," Travis said. "If she did, I'm certain she'd be out of here quicker than Elaine. Sooner or later, she'll get tired of the dust and isolation and the endless work. She'll move on."

"Looks like she's enjoyin' the dust to me," Snake said. "And she's the one who decided she needed to learn how to ride. I put her on that little dappled mare. I thought that would be a good horse for her. She's a nice little lope horse. And I found Josie a saddle, but I had to do some quick riggin' with the stirrups. Her legs ain't as long as yer average ranch hand's. Next time you go into town you might want to find her somethin' a little nicer, maybe with some purdy hand toolin' and a few fara-diddles."

"She's not staying, Snake."

"I thought I might start teachin' her how to cook. You know I've been hopin' to take a little trip to Paris before I hang up my rope. But I can't leave Castle Creek without findin' someone to cook."

"There's any number of hands I could hire to cook."

"But none of 'em are as pretty as Josie, now, are they?"

"Why are you so determined to drive us to the altar?"

"Why are you so determined to drive her away?" Snake asked. "This ranch needs a woman's touch."

"Not when everything she touches turns to disaster."

"She's a good woman," Snake said.

"Then you marry her," Travis said.

Snake pushed away from the fence. "Nah. I think she favors you." He nodded in Josie's direction. "She's ready to try a higher gear. Maybe you can give her a few pointers." Snake headed toward the house, leaving Travis to his own thoughts.

Travis watched her for a few minutes more. She hadn't even noticed he was there yet, so focused was her attention on her riding. He backed away from the corral and retrieved Red, then swung up into the saddle. Bending down, he unhitched the gate and maneuvered his horse into the corral.

He rode up beside her and pulled the gray to a stop. She turned her gaze up to his. Her eyes were bright with excitement and she graced him with a blindingly beautiful smile.

"Hi," she cried. "I'm learning to ride." She reminded him of a child on Christmas morning, so full of exhilaration and amazement. He was tempted to scoop her into his arms and kiss her right then, taking full advantage of her excitement before she had a chance to refuse him. He tried to brush the thought from his mind, but it stubbornly lingered as his gaze dropped to her mouth.

"I can see that," Travis said. "Snake says you're ready to try something a little faster."

She crinkled her nose apprehensively and he noticed a sprinkling of freckles across her sunburned face. "I—I'm not sure, I'm—"

"You're ready," Travis said. "Come on."

She followed him out of the corral and into the yard, then pulled the mare to a halt.

He wheeled his horse around and stopped beside her. Reaching out, he covered her gloved hands with his as she gripped the saddle horn. Even through the two layers of leather, the touch was electric. "Don't be afraid," Travis said. "Your horse will be able to sense that. A lope is like a slow gallop and much smoother than a trot, so it will be easier. You'll just be moving a little faster, that's all."

"I—I'm not afraid," Josie said, slipping her fingers from beneath his and raising the reins.

He pulled his hands away, the feel of her fingers still imprinted on his. "Then give her a soft kick and let's go," he challenged.

Josie drew a deep breath and forced a smile. Then she pushed her hat onto her head and jabbed her heels into the horse's side. Travis watched as she took off toward the west. At first he thought she might pull up and slow the horse, but then she adjusted herself to the new gait. By the time she reached the edge of the yard, she looked comfortable in the saddle.

He slapped Red with the reins and rode out after her. They rode side-by-side in an easy gallop for at least a mile, Travis keeping an eye on her the whole time. He was amazed at how incredibly beautiful she looked with the wind blowing through her long hair—and how well she rode. She had to have strong legs to put up with the abuse that riding delivered to a tenderfoot's body, but she seemed to be a natural on horseback.

"Are you sure you've never ridden before?" he shouted.

Josie slowed her horse to a walk and he responded in kind. "Never," she replied, breathless. "But I already love it. Snake says he's going to teach me how to work the herd. He says with a little practice I'll be able to control Shadow with my knees. Then I won't need to hold on to the reins."

"Shadow?" Travis asked.

"That's her name. Snake said I could name her if I wanted. He says that she's the perfect horse for me. He fixed the saddle for me, too."

His hands tightened on the reins. It sounded like she and Snake were getting pretty damn close. To hear her tell it, Snake had hung the moon and the stars and ran Castle Creek, to boot. But she was riding Travis's horse, on Travis's saddle, over Travis's land, and he deserved at least a portion of her warmth and affection.

"Did you see Clementine today?" Josie asked. "She's getting so cute."

Travis glanced over at her. "Clementine?"

"Winnie's baby. I named her after Clementine. You know, 'Oh, my darlin', oh, my darlin', oh, my darlin' Clementine.' Snake taught me the song. It's about mining. It reminded me of our trip to Bisbee." She gave him a wide-eyed look. "We can keep her, can't we? I mean, I know it's not right to name the animals, but I didn't think there was much chance that we'd have to eat her."

"Not too long ago, you wanted to make Winnie into a stew."

"Winnie and I have come to an understanding," Josie said. "I think we'll get along much better now."

They rode on in silence, Travis stealing a look at her every so often. She'd carved out a place for herself in his heart and now she was carving out a place on Castle Creek. He wanted to believe that she might want to stay, but he couldn't allow himself such unbridled optimism. Her enthusiasm for riding and ranching would wane sooner or later. And then she'd leave him alone, with all the animals she'd named.

Besides, what kind of security could he offer her? The ranch teetered on the edge of bankruptcy now and things wouldn't improve overnight, even if they did have a good roundup. She'd expect a comfortable life with money to buy the things women liked to buy. And he wanted to give her all those things and more. But he couldn't—not now and maybe not ever.

So why did that make him so angry? What difference did it make? Unless, of course, he really wanted a future with her... which he didn't. Shoot, why would he want a future with her? Unless, of course, he loved her. Which he—

"Maybe we should head back," Travis blurted.

Disappointment colored her gaze, but she nodded anyway. "Maybe we should," she said softly. "I've still got some chores to do. I got a little wrapped up in the riding lessons. I'm sorry."

Travis watched a dark curl blow against her damp temple. He could almost feel the silky strand between his fingers and fought the urge to reach out and tuck it behind her ear. "You ride well," he murmured. "I'm surprised. I didn't realize you were such a good athlete."

She smiled in delight. "Thanks. You want to race back to the house?"

Travis shook his head. "I don't think you're ready for any racing, Josie."

"No?" she teased. "Are you afraid I might beat you?"

He chuckled. Though she looked exhausted, she hadn't lost any of her contrary nature. "No. I'm afraid you might fall off your horse and break your neck."

She shot him a haughty glare. "Would you like to put a little bet on it?"

"Josie, we're not going to race."

"If I win, you promise to give me a riding lesson every evening for the next week. And if you win, I'll . . ." She frowned as she tried to come up with an appropriate wager. "I'll . . ."

"Give Red a bath every evening for a week," Travis said.

Josie's brow quirked up in amusement and she nodded slowly. "All right. It's a bet." Then, with a laugh, she wheeled her horse around and took off toward the ranch house. She wasn't riding fast and Travis could have easily beaten her by urging his mount into a full-out run.

But he didn't try. No matter what she might think, teaching Josie to ride could never be considered a chore. Hell, he'd have agreed to shovel out the chicken coop with a fork to share a week's worth of sunsets with her.

JOSIE SAT on the edge of the tub in Travis's bathroom and trailed her hand lazily through the steaming water. Her nightly bath had always been a source of sublime pleasure and numbing relaxation, driving the cold from her bones and washing the grit from her skin. But she hadn't had a real bath since she'd moved out of the ranch house. Though the copper tub was adequate, it wasn't made for soaking. And right now her sore muscles cried out for a long soak, loud enough for her to risk another trip into the ranch house in the middle of the night.

She hadn't been able to sleep anyway. Beyond the snoring that went on in the bunkhouse, her thoughts constantly turned to Travis. She just couldn't figure him out. In one moment, he acted like he could barely stand to be around her, and in the next, he was fixing a horse race so he could. Was this the same man who had kissed her so passionately that night on the road back from Javelina's?

Josie reached over and turned off the water, then drew a deep breath and listened to the silence all around her. She had turned the lights off in the bathroom and the only illumination came from a small night-light near the sink. She closed her eyes and tipped her head back.

What did he want from her? She'd tried to fit in, but he still wasn't happy with her. She could see it every time she looked into his eyes—he'd meet her gaze and then he'd deliberately look away. He'd become tense and distant and then he'd find some excuse for escaping her presence.

She bit back a frustrated groan. And the more distant he became, the more restless she felt. Maybe if she knew what *she* wanted, then what *he* wanted wouldn't matter so much. Right now, she wanted to sink into a tubful of hot water. She wanted to close her eyes and forget all the confusing and conflicting feelings that seemed to torment her lately.

At first it had all seemed so simple. She'd stay at Castle Creek until she figured out what she was going to do for her fantasy life. But somewhere along the line her life at Castle Creek had become her fantasy. She wanted to stay and make a difference here, to watch all Travis's dreams come true for the ranch.

But she also wanted more. She wanted the man lying tangled in the sheets outside the bathroom door. For the past three nights she'd replayed all her earlier trips to his bathroom—the times she'd walked by his bed and watched him sleep, counting each deep breath he took, imagining the feel of his beard-stubbled face and his soft, rumpled hair beneath her fingers.

And every night she'd fought the temptation to slip back into the ranch house and wake him, to crawl into his bed and wrap herself in his arms. Somehow she sensed she would find a place there, a place where she felt safe and secure and protected from all her fears and doubts, a place where she'd finally find the fulfillment of all her fantasies.

There was no use denying it any longer. She was in love with Travis McKinnon. She had known as much from the first time he had truly kissed her, there on the road as they'd looked at the meadow with its lush grass and its promise for the future. It was then that she had decided to make a place for herself in his world. At first it had been just a job, but all along she had subconsciously hoped that one day he would come to need her as much as she yearned to be needed.

Still, something stood between them, dragging at their desire until it became hopelessly snarled in confusion and uncertainty. How could she know whether her feelings for him were real or just imagined—a convenient excuse for avoiding a life on her own? And how could she judge his feelings for her when he so steadfastly pushed her away?

She stood and stared down at the water. The only way to know would be to leave here, yet the mere thought stabbed at her heart like a knife. She belonged on Castle Creek. But how long could she stand by and take Travis's rejection? A week, a month, maybe a year? Or the rest of her life?

Josie silently kicked off her shoes and slipped out of her jeans. As she distractedly worked the buttons of her flannel shirt open, she heard the soft creak of the bathroom door behind her. She froze, her fingers trembling, afraid to turn around.

Though she sensed his presence, she had no clue to his reaction. Was he surprised to find her here or had he known all along? She slowly turned to face him and met his gaze, a gaze filled not with shock, but with desire.

He had pulled on a pair of jeans, but hadn't bothered to button them. His chest was bare and his skin gleamed in the soft light. He had combed his hair back with his fingers, but it still curled around his face and against his neck.

"I was wondering if you'd ever come back," he murmured.

She shifted nervously. "How . . . how long have you known?" she asked.

"Since the first night," Travis replied.

"Why didn't you say something?"

"I didn't care."

"So you don't want me to leave?"

He didn't answer, but she saw his reply as his gaze skimmed down her body. He wanted her to stay, and for the first time she felt that he might not push her away. Slowly, hesitantly, she reached for the last button on her shirt, then parted the front and shrugged it off her shoulders, standing in front of him unabashedly naked.

His eyes flickered and he drew a sharp breath. And then she took a step toward him. In a heartbeat, he pulled her into his arms and kissed her, his hands and his mouth feverish, demanding, nearly frantic with need.

"God, I can't fight you anymore," he said. "I just can't."

"Then don't," Josie said, shivering beneath his touch.

His hands drifted down to her backside and he pulled her against him. She winced as her sore muscles responded and cursed their horse race back to the house.

"Too much riding?" he asked, tracing a line of kisses along her neck.

"Mmm," she said, nearly forgetting the pain for the feelings he was arousing in her.

"We'll have to fix that." He kissed her long and deep once more, then stepped around her and turned on the shower. She watched as he pushed off his jeans, releasing the full evidence of his arousal. She reached out to touch him, but he took her shoulders and turned her away from him, guiding her into the shower.

The warm water rushed over her, soaking her hair and loosening her tight muscles. She braced her arms against the wall, her buttocks brushing against his hardness as he gently massaged her shoulders. He reached around her and grabbed a sponge, then soaped it.

Slowly he scrubbed her back from her nape to the base of her spine, taking exquisite care to wash every inch of her skin. His arms circled her and he began to lave her neck. As she turned to face him, his gaze dropped to her soap-slicked skin. Grasping her shoulders, he gently pushed her beneath the water, letting it sluice between her breasts. She closed her eyes and an instant later his mouth was on her, hot and teasing, drawing her nipple between his lips until she cried out in surprise at the current that ran through her.

She felt as if she'd been transported to another world where nothing else existed but the touch of his hands and his mouth on her body. She could hear only the water and the soft, encouraging sounds he made, sounds that had no meaning beyond what they shared.

He ran his hands along her torso, then dipped his fingers between her legs. Her breath caught at the jolt of desire that raced through her and she felt as if she would lose consciousness, her legs becoming boneless and her mind swirling with unfocused need.

She reached down to touch him, but he stepped away and out of the shower, only to return a moment later. He sheathed himself, then tossed the torn foil away. With an eager moan, he picked her up, wrapping her legs around his waist and pressing her back against the glass block wall.

She knew what was coming, yet the power and beauty of it was so unexpected that she cried out his name as he entered her. One smooth, sure stroke and then he grew still, the rise and fall of his chest his only movement. Her breathing fell into the rhythm of his and as he began to move again, her body matched every thrust.

His movements became more urgent and her mind focused sharply on the feel of him inside her, against her, around her, but especially at the place where they were so intimately joined. A spiraling tension began to build at her core and she whispered her need, begging him to give her release.

And then it was there, upon her, shattering her control and sending her over the edge. He thrust into her once more, crying out his own fulfillment.

Later, after she'd untangled her legs from around his waist and he'd regained his breath, they refilled the tub and slipped into the warm water. She sat between his legs, her back against his hard chest, and he washed her hair. The whirlpool jets bubbled around them, massaging her body until she fell asleep in his arms.

He woke her up to dry her with soft, fluffy towels, then carried her to the bed and made love to her again. When their passion had finally been sated, she nestled against him and fell asleep again, waking only when the sun began to fill the room with a gray light.

Josie watched him sleep for a long time, then quietly climbed out of bed and retrieved her clothes. She didn't want to leave the warmth of his arms, but she felt compelled to protect what they'd shared. This night was part of a fantasy, a fantasy she didn't want to dissolve in the light of day. She would come to him again in the middle of the night. And maybe, somehow, he'd learn to love her as much during the daylight hours as she knew he did in the dark.

JOSIE STOOD on the bunkhouse porch, her arms braced on the railing as she strained to hear the conversation taking place near the machine shed. She'd missed breakfast and it was nearly lunchtime by the time she'd opened her eyes.

The boys had still been asleep when she'd slipped back into the bunkhouse before dawn, but they'd risen a short time later and she'd listened to them dress from behind her blanket wall. After spending the previous evening unsuccessfully at the task, Newt and Harley set out at dawn with a new plan to rescue Travis's pickup, a plan that required Snake's help and Harley's truck in addition to the tractor.

Now, all four of them were gathered around the back end of Travis's truck, sitting on their heels and discussing the prognosis. None of them looked very happy, a fact that was reinforced when Travis stood, yanked off his hat and kicked it across the ground.

Well, she might as well face the music. Though her disasters had slowed somewhat, they obviously hadn't stopped. But after what they'd shared last night, he might be more inclined to forgive her. She stepped off the porch and wandered toward the shed, picking up traces of the conversation as she approached.

"This is just great," Travis said angrily. "Exactly what I need right now."

"Sorry, boss," Harley said. "But we hitched on the chains and the whole back end just pulled right out. It was busted from the impact, not the tow."

Travis raked his fingers through his hair and cursed vividly. "It's totaled, isn't it?"

All three of the ranch hands nodded. Josie stepped up to the group and they all turned to look at her. One by one, they wandered off in different directions, each one shooting her a sympathetic smile as they left.

"Can't you fix it?" Josie said softly.

He stiffened at the sound of her voice. "It's totaled, Josie," he said, his voice emotionless. "That means it would cost more to fix it than the truck is worth."

"I'd be happy to pay for the repairs," Josie offered.

He turned to her, his jaw tight, his fists clenched. "And how will you do that?"

"I'll work harder and save my paychecks."

"The truck is totaled, Josie. It can't be fixed."

"Well, then, I'll buy you a new one."

Travis laughed harshly. "If I don't have the money to buy a new truck, where am I going to find the money to pay you the extra wages to buy me a new truck?"

"Well, there must be something we can do," Josie cried.

Travis shook his head and closed his eyes, as if trying to control his temper. "I gotta get out of here," he finally said. He turned away from her and started toward the corral.

"Travis, wait," she called. "We need to talk about this!"

"I don't want to talk, Josie. Just leave me alone."

She watched as he retrieved his horse from the corral and pulled a bridle over Red's head. He didn't take time for a saddle, merely pulled himself up on the horse's bare back. Then he kicked the horse in the sides and it bolted, heading out to the southwest at a furious gallop.

Josie watched until they both disappeared behind a rise, a cloud of dust marking their escape. She bit her bottom lip and forced back a flood of tears. She had hoped the night they'd spent together would change things between them, but obviously she'd been wrong. At the first sign of trouble, he'd pushed her away.

Well, she wasn't going to let him do it again! If they couldn't talk about their problems, what hope did they have for any kind of future together? And she wanted a future with him. Last night had made her sure of that.

With single-minded resolve, Josie strode to the tack shed and found her saddle. Shadow was in the corral and came up to her as soon as she stepped inside the gate. She methodically saddled and bridled the horse, taking care to follow each of Snake's specific steps. It took her much longer than she expected, but when she swung up on Shadow's back, she realized that the time spent was worth it. Unlike her two tries the previous day, this time the saddle didn't slide sideways under her weight.

Her muscles still ached from yesterday's ride, but she steeled herself against the pain and nudged the horse into an easy gallop. If she was going to be uncomfortable, she might as well get it over with as fast as she could.

She followed the same path she'd driven with the truck, but the horse covered the ground much more easily. As she approached the creek bed, she turned Shadow to the west and headed toward the line cabin. Somehow she knew she'd find him there and wasn't surprised to find Red tethered out front.

The door to the cabin was open and she walked inside. He stood with his back to her, his arms braced against the wood stove, his head bent. He'd heard her entrance for she saw him stiffen slightly and his hands tighten on the edge of the stove.

"You can't just keep running away from me," Josie said softly.

"Would you prefer that I scream and shout at you?" he asked, refusing to face her.

She placed her hand on his shoulder and felt the muscles grow taut beneath her fingers. "If that's what you want to do, yes. At least you'd be honest about your emotions. But this isn't honesty, Travis—it's avoidance. I should know. I spent my whole life avoiding the truth, deluding myself into believing that I couldn't change anything. I'm sorry about the truck. That's all I can say. If you can't get over it, then there's not much chance that we'll have a future together."

He turned to her, his pale gaze cold. "You want honesty? I don't give a damn about the truck."

She blinked in confusion. "Then why are you so angry?"

He grabbed her shoulders. "*That's* why I'm angry. Because I don't give a damn about the truck. I don't give a damn about this ranch. I don't give a damn about anything but you anymore." He snatched his hands from her shoulders as if he'd been burned. "And that's the hell of it all."

"I—I don't understand," Josie said.

He closed his eyes and tipped his head back, then drew a deep breath. "This ranch used to mean everything to me and now it's just standing between me and what I want." He looked down at her, a pained expression on his handsome face. "I want you, Josie. I think about you night and day. But you don't belong here. You deserve more."

Josie reached out and wove her fingers through his. His anger and uncertainty overwhelmed her, twisting at her heart until it ached. "But I don't want more. I want this."

He laughed bitterly and tugged out of her grasp, then turned away. "Forgive me if I don't believe you, but I've heard that before."

"You haven't heard it from me," Josie said. "And I'm not Elaine."

Travis spun around and glared at her. "Oh, no? Well, then, who are you? 'Cause I don't know. I don't know where you come from or what you've been. I don't know anything about you, and yet I'm willing to give this all up just to provide a life for you." He raked his hands through his hair. "All I've ever wanted was this ranch and now it's not enough."

"Yes, it is," she protested.

He shook his head, his expression filled with self-disgust. "I've even considered returning to Chicago. I've got a multimillion-dollar company waiting for me there. We'd live in luxury, you'd have anything your heart desired. Hell, we'd be rich."

"All I want is you," she said softly.

He ignored her words. "Instead, all I've got to offer you is a half-bankrupt ranch and a future filled with hard work and no guarantee of a payoff. I'm not going to let you to make that choice, Josie. You'll only regret it later on."

Tears burned at the corners of her eyes, but she fought them with all her will. "Travis stop talking like this."

"Why? Does it scare you? Because it should."

"No! A future with you doesn't scare me."

"Well, it scares the hell out of me, Josie. You scare the hell out of me and I don't know what to do about it." He cursed softly and turned away. "Just go. Get out of here before I make love to you again."

"I'm not leaving. I love you, Travis."

He glanced over at her and laughed bitterly. "It seems you'll say anything to keep a job."

"I love you," she repeated.

"Unfortunately, love won't pay the bills." His mouth curved cynically.

"I know you love me, Travis. And someday you'll realize it and then you'll know how I feel. You'll know why these things don't make a difference."

He walked away from her, retreating to the other side of the room. "Just go, Josie, and leave me alone."

She closed her eyes and drew a deep breath. "Is that really what you want?"

"Yes," he said.

Josie drew on every shred of courage she had, then turned and walked out the door. She barely had the strength to pull herself up onto Shadow's back, but did it anyway. All her energy had suddenly deserted her, drained from her at his demand for solitude. She nudged the horse into a slow gallop and let Shadow find her own way home.

The ride passed in a blur of hurt and anger and frustration, but she held her tears inside, a trick she'd learned well as a child. He could not drive her away, she wouldn't let him. Yet she didn't have the heart to fight him anymore.

As Josie came over the last rise she stopped Shadow and gazed down at the ranch house below. To an outsider it might look rundown and shabby, but she'd come to love Castle Creek as much as Travis did. As she scanned the yard her eyes were caught by an odd sight. She put her hand to her forehead to block the sun and stared down at the long black limousine parked in front of the ranch house.

With a groan she slapped the reins against Shadow's neck and started toward the house. When she reached the yard, she slid off the horse's back and looped the reins around the hitching rail. Snake, Newt and Harley stood on the bunkhouse porch, watching the limousine suspiciously. Snake moved to step off the porch but Josie held out her hand to stop him.

Slowly she approached the car, then knocked on the reflective-glass window. A soft whir sounded as the electric panel lowered.

"Hello, Mother," she said. "How did you find me?"

The door swung open. "Get in, Josephine."

Josie turned to take a last look around the ranch, committing every detail to memory. Then she waved to the boys and stepped into the limo, closing the door on her life at Castle Creek for good.

# 9

"WHITES, COLORS, delicates. Don't mix colors with whites, especially darker colors like red or blue because they'll run. Wash the colors in cold, the whites in warm."

"Keep the reds separate," Josie repeated. Her memory flashed back to Travis's pink underwear and she smiled at her mother's housekeeper, Hester. "I knew that one already."

Hester nodded encouragingly. "See, this isn't so difficult, Miss Josie. You're picking it all up quite quickly."

"I have a good teacher," Josie said. "And I want to thank you for helping me out with this, Hester. Maybe this afternoon, after I take my driver's test, we can tackle ironing?"

"What is going on in here?" Evelyn Eastman stood in the doorway of the laundry room, her lips pursed distastefully. She wore a floor-length silk robe. Though she'd just risen from bed an hour before, her hair was immaculately arranged and her makeup artfully applied. She was approaching sixty, but a series of face-lifts, a stringent diet, and plenty of sleep kept her looking much younger.

Though her mother chose to sleep late, Josie had been up since sunrise. Strange, how she still operated on ranch time. "Hester is teaching me how to do laundry,"

Josie explained, sorting through the piles of dirty clothes and linen.

Her mother sighed dramatically. "Josephine, I wish you would stop with this silliness. You were not put on this earth to do laundry. You were born to be a figure skater. And, Hester, I would appreciate it if you wouldn't encourage her. First you have her vacuuming and then I catch her waxing the bathroom floor, and now the laundry. Really, I can't tell you how this upsets me."

"I'm sorry, ma'am, but—"

"You don't have to apologize, Hester," Josie said as she filled the washer with dirty laundry. "My mother still believes she can control my life. If I want to do laundry, I can damn well do laundry."

"Oh, isn't that lovely talk?" her mother admonished. "Is that what you learned on that odious ranch? To curse like some common sailor?"

Josie closed the lid and flipped on the machine. Her mother was baiting her, expecting a show of high temper or at least a small hissy fit, something she could deal with in her usual domineering manner. But Josie's temperamental behavior was a thing of the past. She had lost her taste for dramatic tantrums somewhere between Tucson and her last day at Castle Creek. Instead of a harsh retort, Josie merely smiled indulgently at her mother. "No," she teased. "I curse like a common cowboy."

"Don't be impertinent!" Evelyn said.

She giggled. "And don't be such a snob, Mother."

"A snob? It doesn't take a snob to recognize the horrible conditions you were living under at that ranch. If it weren't for that Chase Mitchell fellow seeing your picture in the Tucson paper, I never would have found you. You'd still be stuck out in the middle of nowhere with those awful men. One of them even had an eye patch. Can you believe that, Hester? He looked like a . . . a pirate."

"His name is Snake, Mother, and he is a kind and caring man. And he isn't a pirate. In fact, when he was young, he was a twister. That's what they call the bull riders in a rodeo. He lost his eye when he got kicked . . . in the head . . . by a bull. That's why he took up calf roping. He was a champion calf roper before he started working at Castle Creek. Now he's a wonderful chef."

"How very interesting," her mother replied, sounding as if she'd just discovered a dead fish in her authentic Sheraton sideboard.

"Snake taught me how to milk a goat."

Evelyn gasped and pressed her palm to her chest. "You touched a barnyard animal?"

"It's a little hard to milk a goat without touching her . . . though I did try that once."

Evelyn shook her head. "Hester, I want you to call Dr. Lerner and make an appointment for our Josephine. Heaven knows what awful germs she picked up."

"You don't have to do that, Hester," Josie countered. "I'm perfectly healthy."

Her mother straightened her spine and fixed her daughter with a haughty glare. "Hester, would you please fix a fresh pot of coffee for me? We'll be having two guests at lunch. Be ready to serve at one. Mrs. Harrington and her son, the dermatologist, will be joining Josephine and me."

Josie touched Hester's elbow. "I can fix the coffee, Hester. I believe my mother wants to have another one of her little chats with me. Probably about my countermanding her orders in front of the help. Come on, Mother, let's get it over with so I can get on with my day." Josie turned and started toward the kitchen. "A dermatologist for lunch? An investment banker for dinner a few nights ago, and a corporate attorney last weekend. How many men will you trot through this house before you realize that I'm not interested?"

"I suppose if I trotted some smelly old cowboy in front of you, you'd be happy?"

Josie's smile faded. "That would depend on the cowboy," she murmured. An image of Travis McKinnon drifted through her mind and she held it there for a long moment. Though they'd been apart for nearly a month, she still dreamed of him every night, imagined the touch of his hands on her body. Though she wanted to think there would be other men in her future, she couldn't seem to see past Travis. He was the first man she had ever loved . . . and maybe the last.

Since she'd arrived back home, she'd thrown herself into learning the basics of everyday living. She'd convinced herself that she was being practical, but deep down inside she knew that she needed to prove something to herself. If she could only put her life together, maybe there would be a chance. . . .

Josie gripped the edge of the counter and tried to banish the hope she felt. She couldn't go back, no matter how hard she tried to turn herself into the kind of person he needed. He didn't want her; he'd made himself perfectly clear. And the sooner she accepted that fact, the better.

She glanced up and watched as her mother sat down in the breakfast nook. Evelyn worried the lacy sleeves of her robe with her perfectly manicured nails, then folded her hands in front of her, waiting patiently to be served her morning coffee. "David called again last night after you went to bed," she said. "He told me the new girl just isn't working out in the Cinderella role. And Misha misses you terribly. They want you back, darling."

Josie scooped coffee into the basket then poured a pot of cold water into the top of the coffeemaker. "I'm not going back, Mother."

She groaned dramatically. "Don't be ridiculous! Of course you're going back."

"No," Josie emphasized. "I'm not. I told you when you brought me here that I wasn't going to live my life by your rules anymore. Skating is your life, not mine."

Evelyn tossed up her hands in frustration. "Fine. I'm a bad mother. I've sacrificed everything for you and now you have the nerve to be—"

"Stop with the guilt. You sacrificed everything for *you*, Mother, not for me. This was your fantasy I was living, not mine."

"And what do you plan to do with your life?" she asked in an accusatory tone. "What big fantasy do you have waiting for you?"

Josie shrugged. "I don't know. I'll find a job, get an apartment. My life will be whatever I choose to make it—it will be mine."

"And what are you qualified to do?" Evelyn prodded.

Josie thought about it for a moment then grinned. "Housework. There must be plenty of people looking for domestic help. Or maybe I could get a job at one of the stables working with the horses. I can clean the stalls, feed the animals, and I can ride, you know. Maybe I could even exercise them." She paused. "After this afternoon, I'll be able to drive, too. I could even deliver pizzas."

Josie's mother moaned and rubbed her temples with her fingertips. "You're trying to kill me, aren't you? You might as well stick a knife in my back. My daughter, cleaning animal stalls and delivering pizzas. I might as well give up all my friends, my clubs, all my charities, and move to another state." She pressed her palm against her chest again, as if what she was about to say caused her great pain. "If you need money, I'll give it to you. Just don't humiliate me by working some common job."

Josie grabbed a pair of coffee mugs and slammed them down on the counter. "I don't want your money."

"I wouldn't give you *my* money. I'd give you *your* money.

"My money?" Josie asked. "What do you mean? I don't have any money."

"Yes, you do. You have a trust fund that becomes yours when you turn twenty-five."

Josie frowned and shook her head in disbelief. "I turned *thirty* last week," she said. "Where did this money come from?"

Evelyn gave her an elegant shrug. "Some of it from the product endorsements you did before you turned eighteen. A lot of it from my parents. And the rest from your father, that two-timing—" She drew a deep breath through her nose and her nostrils flared. "I'd say it, but I don't use that kind of language."

Josie rounded the counter and took a seat at the table. "Why didn't you tell me?" she asked, forcing her mother to meet her gaze.

"Because I didn't think you were ready to know. You hadn't grown up enough to handle such a large sum of money."

"How large, Mother?" Josie demanded.

"Large enough," Evelyn said. "You know it is perfectly rude to discuss money."

"How large, Mother?" Josie said, enunciating each word. "Large enough for me to pay the rent on an apartment?"

"Large enough for you to buy one of those smelly old ranches, I'd suspect." Her mother sighed. "There's close to a quarter million."

"Dollars?" Josie gasped.

"Of course, dollars. What else?"

Josie closed her eyes and shook her head. "I can't believe you kept this from me." She clenched her fists, then fixed Evelyn with a penetrating glare. "This is just another one of your control tactics. Can you understand why I'm doing this now? It's because of this type of dictatorial interference in my life."

Evelyn waved her hand, brushing off Josie's statement. "Please, darling, let's at least be honest here. What would you have done five years, even six months ago, if I'd told you about the money? You probably would have spent it all. A quarter of a million is not that much."

Josie frowned as she considered her mother's statement. Maybe she was right. She probably would have walked off the rink then and there and gone on a yearlong shopping spree. In the end, it would have been gone and she probably would never have set foot on Castle Creek. "All right. Maybe I would have wasted it, but you still should have told me."

"I didn't think you were ready to know. And I am the executor of the trust, so I'm in charge."

"But why give up your control now? Why not keep it a secret even longer?"

Evelyn looked directly into Josie's inquiring gaze. "Because, whether I want to admit it or not, you've changed." A melancholy tone tinged her words. "I'm not sure why or how, but you're different. You're not the daughter I raised." She laughed dryly. "That's probably a good thing, you know. I'm not sure I understand who you're becoming, but at least you are showing some maturity and character."

"You should have told me sooner," Josie said softly. "It could have made a difference. I could have at least paid him back."

Her mother reached out and covered Josie's hands with hers. Josie glanced down and studied her mother's long fingers. She couldn't recall the last time her mother had shown her even the slightest gesture of affection beyond a very proper and dry peck on the cheek. She pulled her hand from beneath her mother's and wove their fingers together distractedly.

"Josephine, I don't know what happened to you on that awful ranch, and I'm not sure I want you to tell me the details. All I know is when you were missing, I was sure I'd never see you again. I know I've made mistakes and I thought your running away was my punishment."

"Mother, I don't want to punish you. The past is past. You did what you thought would make me happy and I had some wonderful opportunities."

"But you're not happy now, are you?"

Josie drew in a sharp breath and forced a smile. "I'm as happy as I can be."

Her mother stood and went to pour herself a cup of coffee. She stared down into her cup. "If you miss it so much, why don't you go back?"

Josie's eyes widened in surprise. "Go back?"

Evelyn clutched the coffee mug in her hand. "Please, don't ask me to say it again. I simply can't believe I said it in the first place."

"I can't go back," Josie murmured. "He doesn't want me there."

Evelyn sat back down at the table. "Who is this 'he,' Josephine?" She reached over and placed her fingers under Josie's chin, then tipped her head up.

"Travis," Josie said, suddenly realizing that this was the first time she'd spoken his name out loud since she'd left. "Travis McKinnon." The sound of his name lingered in her mind like a favorite tune almost forgotten.

"Are you in love with this boy?"

Josie smiled. "He's not a boy, Mother. He's thirty-seven years old. And yes, I guess I am in love with him."

Evelyn sighed. "Oh, dear. I was afraid of that."

"You know, when I first met him, I was sure you'd hate him, and that made me even more attracted to him. But after I got to know him, I realized I'd been wrong. I mean, I was still attracted to him, but because of something else. He's got this incredible strength and determination about him, like he could accomplish anything he set his mind to. And he made *me* feel that way, too."

"He sounds like a good man, Josephine."

Josie smiled at her mother's grudging compliment. "He really is, Mother."

"Well, then, there's only one thing for you to do. You'll have to go back," Evelyn stated, as if there were no other alternative. "I didn't raise you to wallow around in self-pity. If you want this man, then go out there and get him."

Josie took a moment to recover from her surprise, then spoke. "Mother, we are not talking about a skating championship here. Just because I want it, won't make it so. Sports psychology does not apply to love."

"Trust me, darling," she said. "You have my blood running through your veins. If you want something bad enough, you'll find a way to get it."

Josie straightened in her chair and carefully considered her mother's words. She made it sound so simple. Could she get Travis back? Was there really a way?

Or was she simply lost in another fantasy that had no chance of becoming real?

A COLD DRIZZLE had been falling since dawn. Travis pulled up the collar of his duster and adjusted his hat so the water wouldn't run down the back of his neck. The herd surged around him and he directed Red sideways with just a nudge of his knee.

The shout of the ranch hands and the barking dogs could be heard above the gentle rumble of hooves. The sounds were underscored by the baleful lowing between mother cow and lost calf. Four extra hands worked the herd along with Snake, Harley and Newt, cutting out a manageable number of cows and their calves and bringing them in closer to the ranch house. Travis had been particularly fortunate this year that the waddies he'd hired were all experienced young hands who had instinctively guessed what was needed from them.

The area around the house was a hive of activity. When the herd reached the ranch, the livestock would be penned in the corral and then the work would really begin. Each calf would be cut out and dragged to the branding area. There, they would have their ears marked before they were branded, castrated, dehorned and, finally, inoculated. It took about a minute from start to finish before the calf was turned out to its mother.

Though the drizzle was a bother, causing a few slips and slides and a lot of muddy clothes, the work proceeded in an almost automatic fashion, all attention focused on the task at hand. Branding at Castle Creek was still done the traditional way, without the help of a chute and a branding table. Travis had never considered changing to the easier method. He'd been taught to ranch this way by his grandfather and would continue to do so until Castle Creek no longer belonged to him.

Until Castle Creek no longer belonged to him, he mused. Snake, Newt and Harley had taken to watching him surreptitiously as they brought in each group of cattle. Travis suspected they were waiting for some confirmation of the success of this year's roundup, assuring them of good wages for the coming year.

Travis had to admit that the roundup looked good, with a much higher percentage of healthy calves born than the previous year. He'd run a preliminary spread-sheet after the first half of the branding had been completed and the numbers proved his estimates. There would be enough to pay both the mortgage and wages. Castle Creek would belong to him for at least another year and maybe more—barring any unforeseen disasters.

Travis wondered if he really had to qualify every projection of success with such a pessimistic warning. After all, the major source of his disasters had left the ranch nearly a month ago.

He'd returned to the house that day to find Josie gone, swept away by some mysterious woman in a black limousine. Newt and Harley were visibly concerned, but Snake just stared off toward the horizon and nodded, as if he expected such a turn of events. Travis didn't ask for details—he was too proud to admit that she'd ever meant anything to him. So her leaving was never discussed and her name never brought up again, at least not in his presence.

He thought he'd be glad to see her go, glad that he could turn his mind back to what was really important—the ranch. But from the moment he'd found her gone until now, he'd never really stopped thinking about her, never really stopped wondering where she'd gone and who she was with.

He couldn't even pass by the corral without stopping to stare at Shadow, without attempting to conjure up an image of Josie sitting astride the pretty gray mare, her hair blowing in the breeze, her face flushed with excitement. He'd taken a special liking to Clementine, Winnie's kid, visiting the barn every morning to give the little black-and-white goat a handful of corn.

But when he really wanted to remember Josie, he stood in the shower and let the hot water rush over him, closing his eyes to all but the image of her naked in his arms.

Hell, he might as well admit it. He missed her. The ranch wasn't the same without her. When she was around, he used to look forward to each day, anticipating the excitement she seemed to inject into everything she did. Life was never dull with Josie around.

"So, what do you think?"

Travis turned to find Snake riding at his side. He hadn't heard him approach, so lost had he been in his own thoughts. "What do *I* think? I don't know. What do you think?" Travis asked.

"Yer the boss man," Snake countered. "Doesn't much matter what I think."

Travis smiled. They'd played this little game at least three times a day since branding had begun and every time Travis had answered with a noncommittal shrug, saying he wasn't sure what he thought. It was about time to put it to rest.

He pulled Red to a stop and braced his hands on his saddle horn while he contemplated the question. Drawing a deep breath, he nodded slowly. "Well, I think it's looking real good, Snake. I think I'm going to be working Castle Creek for a while yet."

Snake nodded, showing absolutely no emotion. "Glad to hear it." He looked out over the herd. "Yer granddaddy would have been real proud at what you done here, Travis. Real proud."

Travis couldn't help but feel proud himself. Coming from Snake, the compliment was almost as gratifying as if it had come directly from Smilin' Jack. "You can tell Newt and Harley that their jobs are safe. I know they've been worried, but it looks like everything's going to turn out just fine."

Snake gave Travis a sideways glance. "They ain't been worried so much about their jobs as they been worried about you."

"Why would they be worried about me?" Travis asked.

"Ever since the princess left, you been off yer feed. They been waitin' fer you to jest give it up and go fetch her."

"She's the one who left," Travis said.

"Hell, you did most of the pushin'. All that little gal wanted was a place to be and you tried yer best not to give it to her."

"All she wanted was a place to hide. I didn't even know who she was, Snake."

"Her name was Josephine Eastman and she was a figure skater. She won a medal in the Olympics and she skated with an ice show right up until the time she showed up at Castle Creek."

Travis gazed at Snake in disbelief. "How do you know this?"

Snake shrugged. "I seen her skate a few times. And she told me."

"She told you and you didn't tell me?" he shouted.

"She asked me not to."

Travis shook his head and chuckled. "A figure skater. Well, that clinches it, then, doesn't it? I guess there wasn't much here on Castle Creek to hold her interest. Ice is in pretty short supply in the low desert."

"She quit skating," Snake said. "Told me she didn't want to go back. I got the notion that she didn't like it

much when she was doing it. I think she liked ranchin'
a whole lot more."

"So why did she leave?"

"Maybe she didn't have a choice," Snake said point-
edly. "Maybe she didn't have any place left to go." A
long silence hung between them as they both watched
the herd.

"You could go get her," Snake suggested. "She lives
in some fancy mansion in Fairfield, Connecticut. That's
out east."

"I know where that is," Travis said. "And Fairfield,
Connecticut, is a whole lot nicer neighborhood than
Deadwater Gulch, Arizona. Josie's used to a comfort-
able life and I can't give her that, not without leaving
Castle Creek. She wouldn't be happy here."

"How do you know that?" Snake challenged. "Did
you ever ask her what she wanted?"

Travis shrugged.

"I think you oughta ask her before you start puttin'
words in her mouth. Maybe you should think about
takin' a trip out east to do that very thing."

"And maybe you haven't noticed, but I got a roundup
to take care of," Travis said.

"Maybe after the roundup you could go," Snake
countered.

Travis glared at him. "And maybe, if I were you, I'd
let this one go."

Snake adjusted his hat and picked up his reins. "I'll
tell the boys yer considerin' it," he said. With that, the
one-eyed ranch hand spurred his horse into a gallop and
headed for the point position.

Travis swore softly. Now that the subject of Josephine had been broached, he knew it would come up

again and again. Her name would find its way into each breakfast and dinner conversation. He'd be reminded of all the clever things she'd done and said, yet none of her disasters would ever be mentioned. She'd become St. Josephine, Castle Creek's most revered lady, and Travis would play the part of the spoiler, a man too proud to return her to her rightful place.

Why couldn't he bring her back? He was certain he loved her. Hell, he'd known that from the very start, even though he refused to admit it to himself. In fact, he'd never felt as strongly about a woman in his life. She had wrapped herself so tightly around his soul, sometimes he felt as if he couldn't breathe for wanting her.

But still, there was an underlying fear, a fear he felt whenever he contemplated a future with her. Ranching was such a tenuous life with so many ups and downs. He had no idea from year to year whether he'd enjoy success or failure. All he knew was that he didn't want her around if he failed. He didn't want to have to look into her eyes and see regret for loving him and fear for her security.

And that was the bottom line, wasn't it? No matter how confident he felt in his abilities to make Castle Creek a success, he wasn't confident enough to bring her back. It would be years before there was extra money to build her a proper house. Then there were children to consider. He was already concerned about the lack of nearby medical care for Josie, much less for the children they might have. And what about education? The nearest school was at least an hour away. Hell, he didn't even have a phone. Life at Castle Creek was not appropriate for a wife and kids.

He had briefly considered moving back to Chicago and taking his place in his father's company. But returning would be the ultimate failure. He'd be forced to admit that his father had been right about Castle Creek. And though he'd have Josie, he'd be miserable, trapped in some steel-and-glass high rise from nine to five. Sooner or later, it would poison their relationship.

So in the end, he really had no choice at all. He'd remain on Castle Creek, alone. He'd make the ranch work and he'd come to accept that he'd be living like a monk for the rest of his life.

JOSIE SWUNG the truck off the main road and onto the rutted dirt path that lead to Castle Creek's ranch house. She'd been driving for four days, and though she'd just gotten her driver's license four days ago, she already felt as if she'd been behind the wheel her entire life.

At first she'd been apprehensive, not at all sure that she'd succeed in her plan. By the time she'd crossed into Virginia she'd convinced herself that she was making a huge mistake. But as she made her way through Georgia and Alabama and then the endless stretch of Texas, she began to believe that maybe she did have a chance with him.

After all, no matter what objection he raised, she had an answer to counter it. Her first goal would be to get her job back and, once that was done, she hoped, given time, all the other things would fall into place. And she did have three other things going for her—namely Snake, Harley and Newt. If she couldn't convince Travis to hire her back, maybe they could exert a little pressure.

As she drove over the last rise she stopped the truck and looked down on the ranch house. The area inside the corral seemed to be bustling with activity. She squinted her eyes to see what the commotion was, then realized that this must be roundup time. Two extra pickups were parked in the yard and cattle filled the space that was usually reserved for the horses.

Josie drew a deep breath and wrapped her fingers firmly around the steering wheel. She glanced up into the rearview mirror and surveyed her appearance. She'd taken special care with her hair and makeup, wanting to make a stunning first impression. A loose, cotton sundress had been a logical choice of wardrobe, but she now wondered whether jeans and a flannel shirt would have been more appropriate. The dress bared her arms and chest and was quite flowing and feminine. But did she really want to appear so feminine? After all, her first priority was to get her job back.

It was too late to change. Besides, she was only using her dress as an excuse to keep from driving down the hill. She was prepared to face Travis again and now was as good a time as any. The sooner she got to work on making her fantasy life come true, the sooner she'd be back in Travis's arms.

Strange how her fantasy had gradually changed. At first she'd just wanted a life of her own, away from the ice and her mother. But now she wanted something more, something that she could only find on Castle Creek.

Josie put the truck into gear and bumped down the hill toward the house. Her approach went unnoticed and no one came to meet the truck when she parked it in the middle of the yard. Certainly they must have seen her coming. A sliver of anxiety shot through her and she nearly shoved the truck into Reverse to drive back up the hill.

But then she drew another deep breath and calmed herself, marshaling all her resolve. She pushed the door open and jumped out, then carefully smoothed her dress.

The wind swirled the dust around her feet and whipped her loose hair across her eyes. She never thought she'd miss the dust and the wind, but she had. She had missed everything about Castle Creek—the rickety front porch of the ranch house, the hodge-podge collection of weathered buildings, the sharp smell of creosote in the breeze, and the glorious chorus of animal noises that seemed to fill the air around her.

She wandered toward the corral but she could see little. Most of the activity was taking place inside the ramshackle fence. When she reached the gate, she stepped up onto the bottom rail and silently observed the cowboys at work.

It seemed as if chaos reigned. Newt and Harley sat atop their horses and chased a calf. Snake stood over a huge barrel that looked like a barbecue grill. And Travis scribbled something on a clipboard. Four other strangers were working at tasks she didn't recognize.

Newt noticed her first, pulling his horse to a stop to stare in her direction. Harley shouted at the boy, then followed Newt's gaze and also reined his mount. Snake was next to see her, and then, one by one, the other hands. All the activity in the corral ground to a dead halt. Travis was the last person to look up.

She wasn't prepared for the shock of his gaze meeting hers. His pale blue eyes were colored with disbelief, yet he didn't look away. He stared at her as if he were absorbing the sight, not certain she was real.

"Shadin' time!" Snake shouted.

Slowly the men dropped their work and headed toward the gate. Each of the hired hands tipped their hat to her as they passed.

Newt smiled broadly and clutched his hat to his chest. "It's good to have you back, Yer Highness."

Harley was next. He gave her a friendly kiss on the cheek. "It's about time," he murmured. "This place has been downright dull since you left."

And finally Snake greeted her. "Yer lookin' mighty fetchin', Princess."

"Thanks, Snake," she replied, giving him a hug.

A blush crept up his weathered cheeks. "You back to stay?"

"I hope so. Wish me luck."

Josie looked back inside the corral. Travis stood rooted in the same place, his clipboard still clutched in his gloved hands. His hat shaded his eyes, but his gaze pierced the shadow of the brim like a laser. He was covered with dust from head to toe and his shirt was unbuttoned, his chest slick with sweat.

Without taking his eyes from her, he dropped his clipboard and tugged off his gloves. They fell into the dust behind him. Then he tipped his hat back on his head and wiped the sweat from his brow with his bandanna.

She wasn't sure whether she should speak or wait for him to say something. "Hello" would be a start, but he hadn't even ventured that far yet. She forced a smile, hoping that might provide an opening, but he merely continued to stare at her. Finally, after another long minute of silence, she decided to gather her courage and speak.

"How are you?" she asked.

"Fine," he replied, his voice even and direct.

She held her arm out over the gate, dangling the keys to the truck from her finger. "These are yours."

He walked toward her, his expression wary. "You came all the way back here to return a set of keys?"

"No, I came here to *give* you these keys. They belong to that truck over there. It's yours."

Travis frowned, then peered over the top of the gate. "What are you talking about?"

"I bought it to replace the one I broke."

He stared at her as if her nose had just grown a foot. "Josie, that's a brand new truck. Where the hell did you get the money to buy it?"

Josie reached into the pocket of her dress, pulled out her brand-new checkbook and handed it to him. "This is also for you. Your signature is good at the bank."

"I don't understand," he said.

"Consider it a deposit. From now on, whenever I make a mistake that costs money, you can just write a check for it. There's plenty of money in there. And I wrote the first check for the truck."

"Josie, I don't want your money," Travis said, pushing the checkbook back at her.

"Then tell me what you want. Tell me how I can make this right. I want my job back, Travis. I've learned how to cook and clean and I know how to operate the washing machine. I can even load a dishwasher, although you don't own a dishwasher. But if you did, I'd be able to operate it. And you should see me with a vacuum cleaner. I'm a whiz on plush carpeting. I have my driver's license now and you know I can ride and I—"

He placed his finger over her mouth to stop her babbling. "You came all this way to ask for your job back?"

She nodded, wide-eyed. "Mmm-hmm."

He snatched his hand away. "No," he said.

Josie's jaw dropped. "No? What do you mean, no?"

"I mean no," Travis said.

"Why not?"

"I don't need a reason. I'm the boss man, and if I say no, it's no."

"But you *have* to give me a reason. I can't argue with you if you don't. I have this all thought out, and I've covered all the possible problems. It can't be money, I've given you all I have. And I can do the job now, so you should have no complaints about that. So what is it?"

Travis raised his brow. "Don't you know?"

"No!" Josie paused, then bit her lower lip. "Unless . . ." She drew a deep breath. "I guess maybe there is one reason left. You can't stand to have me around." She tipped her chin up defiantly and forced back a flood of tears. Coming here had been a mistake, she knew that now. "I—I'll just be going. I'm sorry to have bothered you."

She began to turn away and then he stopped her. He placed his palm on her cheek and murmured her name. Slowly she brought her gaze back to his. His eyes were ablaze with need and a warm smile curled his lips.

"I don't want you to go," he said, his voice catching in his throat. "But I can't ask you to stay."

"Why not?"

His jaw tightened in frustration. "Because the only way I'll let you stay is if you marry me," Travis said. "And I can't ask you to do that."

A skeptical smile broke across Josie's face and she laughed. "You want me to marry you? You won't give me a job, but you're asking me to *marry* you?"

"No," he replied. "I mean, I would ask you if I had more to offer. But this is it, Josie. I've got a run-down ranch that's mortgaged to the hilt and a pretty shaky future at best. It's going to be hard work and even then I can't give you the things I want to give you."

Josie stared at him for a long moment, then shook her head in disgust. "Travis McKinnon, you are a crock-headed saddle stiff. You have all the sense of a hinny in a haybarn. And I wouldn't be surprised if the Lord poured your brains in with a teaspoon and then jiggled your arm."

"What's your point, Josie?" he said.

"I don't want anything but this," she cried. "This is all I've ever wanted. I love Castle Creek, Travis. And I love you. I want to be with you. I want to plant grass and watch it grow. I want to watch the sun set from the west pasture. And I want to have your babies and make a family for you."

Travis clenched his jaw as if he were fighting his own best judgment. Then he grabbed her hands and climbed up on the gate. "You know what you're getting into?" he asked. "Have you really thought this through?"

"Absolutely," she replied. "And what about you? Do you know what *you're* getting into?"

He grinned. "Absolutely."

"Then ask me again, cowboy."

He cupped her face in his hands and stared deep into her eyes. "Marry me, Princess. I love you more than life itself and I promise I'll do everything in my power to make you happy."

Josie threw her arms around his neck. "Yes," she shouted. "I will marry you!"

He kissed her long and deep and then gazed into her eyes. Josie knew at that moment that whatever fantasies she might have had about Travis McKinnon and a life on Castle Creek were all just that—fantasies. The love she felt for Travis, and for the land he cherished, was not a fantasy, but very real and meant to last a lifetime.

*Do you have a secret fantasy?*

Ashleigh Frost does. Shy and straitlaced, she'd spent her life being controlled first by domineering parents and then by a no-good husband. All she wants to do now is have a little fun—and fantasy. To bring strong-willed men to their knees, weak from their desire for her. Only then she meets Detective Cade Hawkins and the sparks threaten to singe her. Experience the seduction in Tiffany White's NAUGHTY BY NIGHT in August 1995.

*Everybody* has a secret fantasy. And you'll find them all in Temptation's exciting new yearlong miniseries, Secret Fantasies. Beginning January 1995, one book each month focuses on the hero or heroine's innermost romantic desires....

# Take 4 bestselling love stories FREE

## Plus get a FREE surprise gift!

---

## Special Limited-time Offer

**Mail to Harlequin Reader Service®**

3010 Walden Avenue
P.O. Box 1867
Buffalo, N.Y. 14269-1867

**YES!** Please send me 4 free Harlequin Temptation® novels and my free surprise gift. Then send me 4 brand-new novels every month, which I will receive before they appear in bookstores. Bill me at the low price of $2.44 each plus 25¢ delivery and applicable sales tax, if any.* That's the complete price and a savings of over 10% off the cover prices—quite a bargain! I understand that accepting the books and gift places me under no obligation ever to buy any books. I can always return a shipment and cancel at any time. Even if I never buy another book from Harlequin, the 4 free books and the surprise gift are mine to keep forever.

142 BPA AJHR

| | | |
|---|---|---|
| Name | (PLEASE PRINT) | |
| Address | Apt. No. | |
| City | State | Zip |

This offer is limited to one order per household and not valid to present Harlequin Temptation® subscribers. *Terms and prices are subject to change without notice. Sales tax applicable in N.Y.

**HARLEQUIN®**

Don't miss these Harlequin favorites by some of our most distin-
guished authors!
And now, you can receive a discount by ordering two or more titles!

| | | | |
|---|---|---|---|
| HT #25559 | JUST ANOTHER PRETTY FACE<br>by Candace Schuler | $2.99 | ☐ |
| HT #25616 | THE BOUNTY HUNTER<br>by Vicki Lewis Thompson | $2.99 U.S./$3.50 CAN. | ☐ |
| HP #11667 | THE SPANISH CONNECTION<br>by Kay Thorpe | $2.99 U.S./$3.50 CAN. | ☐ |
| HP #11701 | PRACTISE TO DECEIVE<br>by Sally Wentworth | $2.99 U.S./$3.50 CAN. | ☐ |
| HR #03268 | THE BAD PENNY by Susan Fox | $2.99 | ☐ |
| HR #03340 | THE NUTCRACKER PRINCE<br>by Rebecca Winters | $2.99 U.S./$3.50 CAN. | ☐ |
| HS #70540 | FOR THE LOVE OF IVY<br>by Barbara Kaye | $3.39 | ☐ |
| HS #70596 | DANCING IN THE DARK<br>by Lynn Erickson | $3.50 | ☐ |
| HI #22196 | CHILD'S PLAY by Bethany Campbell | $2.89 | ☐ |
| HI #22304 | BEARING GIFTS by Aimée Thurlo | $2.99 U.S./$3.50 CAN. | ☐ |
| HAR #16538 | KISSED BY THE SEA<br>by Rebecca Flanders | $3.50 U.S./$3.99 CAN. | ☐ |
| HAR #16553 | THE MARRYING TYPE<br>by Judith Arnold | $3.50 U.S./$3.99 CAN. | ☐ |
| HH #28847 | DESIRE MY LOVE by Miranda Jarrett | $3.99 U.S./$4.50 CAN | ☐ |
| HH #28848 | VOWS by Margaret Moore | $3.99 U.S./$4.50 CAN | ☐ |

**(limited quantities available on certain titles)**

| | | |
|---|---|---|
| | **AMOUNT** | $ |
| **DEDUCT:** | **10% DISCOUNT FOR 2+ BOOKS** | $ |
| | **POSTAGE & HANDLING** | $ |
| | ($1.00 for one book, 50¢ for each additional) | |
| | **APPLICABLE TAXES*** | $ _____ |
| | **TOTAL PAYABLE** | $ _____ |
| | (check or money order—please do not send cash) | |

To order, complete this form and send it, along with a check or money order for the
total above, payable to Harlequin Books, to: **In the U.S.:** 3010 Walden Avenue,
P.O. Box 9047, Buffalo, NY 14269-9047; **In Canada:** P.O. Box 613, Fort Erie, Ontario,
L2A 5X3.

Name: _____

Address: _____ City: _____

State/Prov.: _____ Zip/Postal Code: _____

*New York residents remit applicable sales taxes.
 Canadian residents remit applicable GST and provincial taxes.                    HBACK-JS2

**THREE GROOMS:**
*Case, Carter and Mike*

**TWO WORDS:**
*"We Don't!"*

**ONE MINISERIES:**

# GROOMS ON THE RUN

Starting in May 1995, Harlequin Temptation
brings you an exciting miniseries called

### GROOMS ON THE RUN

Each book (and there'll be one a month for three
months!) features a sexy hero who's ready to say,
"I do!" but ends up saying, "I don't!"

Watch for these special Temptations:

In May, **I WON'T!** by Gina Wilkins #539
In June, **JILT TRIP** by Heather MacAllister #543
In July, **NOT THIS GUY!** by Glenda Sanders #547

Available wherever Harlequin books are sold.

"Bravo! *Love Game* is a superb read, sexy, scintillating and scrumptious!"
—Suzanne Forster

**Explore every forbidden wish and desire…**

# Love GAME
## by MALLORY RUSH

Chris Nicholson is a widow in search of the perfect father for her little girl. She is not looking for a lover. Enter Major Greg Reynolds, an old high school boyfriend who may not be the perfect father, but as a lover he takes Chris down the new paths of fantasy love. Chris has found the perfect lover, but can she risk losing him in search of the perfect father?

Don't miss *Love Game*, available in July wherever Harlequin books are sold.

LG

# As a Privileged Woman, you'll be entitled to all these Free Benefits. And Free Gifts, too.

To thank you for buying our books, we've designed an exclusive FREE program called *PAGES & PRIVILEGES*™. You can enroll with just one Proof of Purchase, and get the kind of luxuries that, until now, you could only read about.

## BIG HOTEL DISCOUNTS

**A privileged woman stays in the finest hotels.** And so can you—at up to 60% off! Imagine standing in a hotel check-in line and watching as the guest in front of you pays $150 for the same room that's only costing you $60. Your *Pages & Privileges* discounts are good at Sheraton, Marriott, Best Western, Hyatt and thousands of other fine hotels all over the U.S., Canada and Europe.

## FREE DISCOUNT TRAVEL SERVICE

**A privileged woman is always jetting to romantic places.** When you fly, just make one phone call for the lowest published airfare at time of booking—or double the difference back! PLUS— you'll get a $25 voucher to use the first time you book a flight AND 5% cash back on every ticket you buy thereafter through the travel service!

HT-PP3A

# FREE GIFTS!

**A privileged woman is always getting wonderful gifts.**
Luxuriate in rich fragrances that will stir your senses (and his). This gift-boxed assortment of fine perfumes includes three popular scents, each in a beautiful designer bottle. _Truly Lace_...This luxurious fragrance unveils your sensuous side. _L'Effleur_...discover the romance of the Victorian era with this soft floral. _Muguet des bois_...a single note floral of singular beauty.

# FREE INSIDER TIPS LETTER

**A privileged woman is always informed.** And you'll be, too, with our free letter full of fascinating information and sneak previews of upcoming books.

# MORE GREAT GIFTS & BENEFITS TO COME

**A privileged woman always has a lot to look forward to.** And so will you. You get all these wonderful FREE gifts and benefits now with only one purchase...and there are no additional purchases required. However, each additional retail purchase of Harlequin and Silhouette books brings you a step closer to even more great FREE benefits like half-price movie tickets... and even more FREE gifts.

_L'Effleur_...This basketful of romance lets you discover L'Effleur from head to toe, heart to home.

_Truly Lace_...
A basket spun with the sensuous luxuries of Truly Lace, including Dusting Powder in a reusable satin and lace covered box.

_Complete the Enrollment Form in the front of this book and mail it with this Proof of Purchase._